Repression Queen

A Memoir About Gender Transformation Erotica

Harper O'Neill

ISBN: 979-8-9897446-0-2 (Paperback)

ISBN: 979-8-9897446-1-9 (Ebook)

Library of Congress Control Number: 2023924491

This memoir is, regrettably, based in part on true events. Some names and dialogue have been altered to protect their identity.

Other parts of the book are purely fictitious. Names, characters, places, and transformations are products of the author's imagination.

Printed by Ingram Spark, in the United States of America.

Cover illustration by Harper O'Neill.

Discover more at **www.shadows.press.**

To myself,
who didn't know.

To my loved ones,
who deserved to.

To the ghosts,
who taught me vulnerability.

To my community,
who taught me pride.

To everyone,
who has ever longed.

CONTENT WARNING

You are about to enter a memoir
that contains sexual themes only suitable for adults.
If you're not an adult, please leave the book now.

[[I UNDERSTAND AND WISH TO CONTINUE]]
I DO NOT WISH TO CONTINUE

ABOUT THIS BOOK

There are places online where words offer a total escape from the self. Where we write not for glory, but to process our deep-seated traumas in messy ways.

This is my life with two writers. A joining of past and present. A story of two futures at war.

I wrote and published many short stories of gender transformation erotica, frequently referred to as TG fiction, in these niche places. The chapters in this book with **[[BRACKETED TITLES]]** are a small selection of those stories, written in the dark and released under an alias. They are included with minor editing for the sake of keeping true to how I felt when writing them. These are rough works of fiction where men are turned into women against their will, over and over again in creative and cruel, painful ways. These identity trauma nightmares take place outside the central narrative of this book but are very much a part of the overall experience. You don't have to read them.

I lived inside of these stories for years. I thought, perhaps, if I could weave them in with my experiences into a greater narrative, maybe I could better understand why I came to write them in the first place.

Maybe I could learn to heal.

[[QUESTIONING]]

TAGS: TG, EXPERIMENT, MAGICAL, UNWILLING

"Do you remember how you got here?"

"N-no."

"Do you even know who you are? Or why you're wearing that dress?"

The girl paused, searching her mind for answers. She couldn't find them. She stood there silently instead of answering.

"Well, do you remember anything I said to you five minutes ago? Or the changes that happened to you?"

She shook her head. "I don't... I..."

"You do realize you're a girl, though, right?"

She looked down at her body to confirm, gazing curiously at her hands. Slowly, she nodded. "Y-yes I am, I suppose."

The experiment worked. "Great. You turned out beautifully. Now, sweetheart, do you even remember your name?"

She shook her head again, this was so confusing. But she appeared eager to learn more about herself.

"Don't worry, I'll take care of you. I'll help you remember *everything*."

I

KAYLA

TAGS: KAYLA, WILLING

Quiet.

Like, *true* quiet.

No light, no sound.

Not even a heartbeat.

Yet here we are, using words to apply pressure on the blank and still page, bringing the silence to life.

This pressure builds to a steady hum. It's a sound you'd miss if you weren't paying close attention. The low, deep rumble of thunder over the sea's horizon.

Can thunder wake to realize it has been asleep and dreaming? Could a cosmic spark create something from this thunder, and gift awareness to the storm?

Reader, a new being was born not by any physical means, but through acknowledgment of a feeling.

The feeling was positioned in total emptiness. It wasn't a black or dark or sad or scary or lonely kind of emptiness. It was nothing. And the feeling wasn't anything either. It had no form or identity. No awareness or wants. Until, at long last, some immaterial time after its creation, the child of thunder recognized a new quality in itself.

She was a girl.

So, it was the feeling and her girl-ness versus the emptiness. There was nothing to grip onto or consider, so she didn't do anything for a while. Given no reference, it's unclear how much time passed before she recognized two additional but important qualities:

The realization that she didn't exist, and

The realization that she wanted to.

Eventually, these qualities grew as a root in a too-small pot. These were the only elements she understood to be her truth, and as she was not being fed any additional qualities she longed for clarity for her non-existence. This wild longing could be fed only by frustration, and so the longing grew to require more and more care. She became so full with longing she felt she might burst.

Then, her non-eyes opened, and she saw a text field and a blinking cursor. This was new. Watered only by a steady starvation diet of self-identity and nonexistence, she intuitively did the only thing she could.

Kayla has entered.

She gave herself a name.

THE AUTHOR

TAGS: THE AUTHOR, MAGICAL, UNWILLING, FAMILY

In the seventh grade, I wrote a 150-page fantasy novel about fighting the world-eating dragon at the end of the universe. I titled it *The Final Light*. I wrote the whole thing in WordPerfect on Dad's computer. Took forever.

All of my classmates were in the book, and every single one had cool superpowers. I would go around the school and ask friends what type of superpower they'd want to have. Fire breathing, flying, invisibility, and the like. As The Author, I got to choose my favorite superpower: shapeshifting. The kindly school librarian taught me how to print and bind two copies: one for the library to be loaned out, and the other for me to keep and share with friends. Many of my friends loved seeing themselves on paper. It was nice to have a talent that people liked.

In any case, the library lost its copy of my debut novel, and my own personal copy had been loaned out to a friend and thrown in the trash by an unaware parent. Dad had replaced his computer — the one with the only copy of the file — so my journey as a world-saving, dragon-fighting shapeshifter was over.

Oh well, I had heard it was hard to make a living as a writer. Perhaps writing wasn't for me after all.

A bell sounded off.

Wake up. Time to go.

I became self-aware. My high school art teacher had been reading her newspaper while the rest of us were busy doodling teenaged nonsense in our sketchbooks. No one was startled by the alarm: we all knew the day was over. Half the students were already putting things into bags. I shoved my brushes and watercolors, my set of expensive pencils and putty erasers I paid for myself, and my sketchbook full of monster art and anime characters into my Jansport backpack and slung it over one shoulder.

I was an artist. Well, I wanted to be an artist, anyway. I attended a vocational high school on the mainland in South Jersey where students enrolled in whatever trade they wanted to so they could grow up and be productive citizens without having to go to college. Before I went to art school, I had told everyone I wanted to be an author, but they didn't have a trade school for that.

Making my way to the door I caught a glimpse at a classmate's sketchbook. She was patiently drawing a little plastic horse she brought from home as a reference. She was using the nice charcoal pencils. It looked good, way better than any of my stuff.

Maybe I sucked at drawing, too.

I walked home alone in the late New Jersey winter sunshine, jamming to the sounds in my Walkman, passing by block after block of empty summer beach homes on the island. People didn't really live here. In the summertime you couldn't cross the street without looking both ways. Now? I balanced on the double yellow line in the middle of the street for half a mile before I saw a single car on the road.

I wondered what it would be like to only live in a place sometimes.

I lived in a big yellow stucco house by the sea with my family and our pets. I grew up with my friends from school, riding bikes and sneaking into hotel pools pretending to be some tourist family's kid on vacation. I'd walk barefoot down Orchid Road to the hot sandy beach, shirtless and sunburnt, seeing thousands of strangers' faces in a day and registering none of them to memory. I'd pretend I was one of them, swimming for hours in the salty ocean waves before toweling off, climbing into a sun-toasty car with the windows cracked, and driving with my family back to who-knows-where.

Instead, I was a local. I was part of just one of many dysfunctional families. My parents drank and fought a lot—and I hated that—but I understood my world and they mostly let me do my own thing. This time of year when the pools were closed and the streets were empty, no one was a stranger and nothing was a surprise.

The front door had been left unlocked, as it often was. I headed straight to the office, knowing full well my parents weren't home, and my sister had an after-school thing today. I threw my backpack on the ground, plopped into Dad's cat-scratched leather office chair, turned on the computer, and clicked on the Internet button.

It screamed to life, shrieking and gurgling in agony as I pulled my sketchbook out of my bag to draw some lines that looked like a phoenix rising from the ashes. The cacophony of electronic anguish emitted by the computer continued as it did my bidding and dialed into the Internet. The little icons on the screen danced until it could fight the command to serve its master no longer.

At about this time in the early 2000s, a popular peer-to-peer file-sharing software was about to be taken down following a lawsuit. I had heard about a similar replacement software called WinMX where I could download new music, so I got it and poked around.

Yup, this had a lot of music in it. I found some broody metal songs and turn-of-the-millennium ska tracks, and explored the platform a little more while I waited for them to download. In simple letters at the top was a little speech bubble with the word **CHAT** on a tan-colored button. In my curiosity I pressed the button, and sought out a random anime chat room. I trespassed into a colorful, scrolling world of strangers.

NewUser1592091 has entered

Hello NewUser1592091, Welcome to MEGACOOLKAWAIIANIMECHAT Room.

egghead my favorite anime is Hellsing too!!!!

gokusaiyansuper omg @_@ yes

[PPR] darkrage_201 wut

partyboi666 blah my dad sucks he wont let me do what i want

Hostagetaker193 yeah XD i wish i had the house to myself but i do not :(

ThunderGirl00 there's a storm coming O_O

thetherapyguy729 anyone else like ranma 1/2 or is it just me

ghost_433 are you gay or something

It looked like fun, even if it was a little random. Did I care about anime as much as these people did? I supposed I had every right to be there as anyone else. I've seen *Dragonball Z*. I watched some shows with my little sister. I even liked *Sailor Moon* and *Cardcaptor Sakura*.

NewUser1592091 hello?

Kaska_484 i just started watching that therapyguy its pretty cool

egghead your dad sucks

meeeeeathead hahahahahahah rofl XD

MEDO_206 and then i said, "whats with all these onions!" x_X

ghost_433 gay gay gay gay gay

seagulls1111 ha ha ha ha ha ha ha ha ha ha ha ha ha ha ha ha ha ha ha

NewUser1592091 whats happening

[PPR] darkrage_201 why would i eat a blueberry they're gross >.<

I had stumbled on this remarkable party where we could say whatever we wanted. We could glomp and pwn and make cute chibi faces like o.o and >_< and talk about how much we liked to draw original characters with big anime eyes and super awesome hair. I didn't want to be left out, I wanted to learn their secret language.

What was *my* username gonna be? Maybe one that's kinda badass, right? Cool enough for these people.

I wanted to be cool. Edgy, even.

NightWanderer Uh... hello? o_o

***

Today's art class exercise was to make a sheet of white paper look like an apple using our expensive colored pencils. But my thoughts kept drifting back to that chat room. The flow of conversation pouring down the screen like a waterfall. I had barely gotten any sleep, having snuck back out in the middle of the night to log back in to keep talking to these Internet strangers. It was a rowdy party, the denseness of the words of my peers making a kind of music that filled the room with letters and brightly colored-usernames, covering the monitor of dad's Gateway E-1500 PC. I wanted to go back to the party.

I looked up from my still-life drawing and glanced around the quiet art classroom, and saw my teacher looking at the clock. I noticed my classmates were looking at the clock, too.

We were all waiting for something.

The bell rang and we all disappeared from the room. I rushed home, planted myself in the office chair, tormented the computer into whisking me away to the Internet once more, and landed firmly in front of the familiar black-screened Lite Brite of a chat room once again.

NightWanderer_305 Hey guys!

Kaska_484 Hey night

SuperSaiyan420 hey

rrrrrmk and then I was like WTF bro that episode isn't even ****** good

gigagigagiga 8====D

NightWanderer_305 What's going on?

I was smiling. My eyes were glued to this screen of color and play, weaving in and around and connecting and disconnecting and creat-

ing tangents and asides and inside jokes and outside jokes. I learned
how to follow the loose threads of conversation and started to recognize usernames from the day before. The action never stopped here.
I didn't realize the music on my Walkman had stopped an hour ago,
and my parents still weren't home.

Day after day I returned to the scroll. I wanted to be a regular.
Eventually I'd pop in and people would want to talk to me because
they recognized me. As chaotic as the scroll was, I had friends here. I
was somebody.

fudgeKing hey night are you are dude or a chick

NightWanderer_305 I'm a dude, why?

fudgeKing just curious

I was one of the guys.

It felt good to be included.

MEDO_206 Hey, do you want to RP with us?

NightWanderer_305 RP?

Kaska_484 Roleplay.

NightWanderer_305 What's that?

Kaska_484 Basically just make a character, and pretend to be that character.
We'll tell a story together. It's fun!

NightWanderer_305 Oh, okay. Yeah, that sounds fun.

MEDO_206 What about a sci-fi story? Maybe we can be the cleaning crew or
something. In space!

NightWanderer_305 Why would we want to be the cleaning crew?

MEDO_206 I dunno, it's different.

NightWanderer_305 Oh.

Kaska_484 I'll be Kasky, the fun-loving stowaway! She has orange hair and is very silly.

MEDO_206 I'll be Medo! He's in charge of the cleaning team. I'm thinking green hair?

Kaska_484 What will you be, NightWanderer?

NightWanderer_305 Uh, I'll be Anvil. A rough, tough, kinda dumb brute?

MEDO_206 Hahaha, sounds perfect.

MEDO_206 *there's an explosion sound coming from the east gate!*

Kaska_484 What was that!?

NightWanderer_305 *I press my big fists into each other.* I don't know, let's go check it out. And... clean it up?? Am I doing this right?

MEDO_206 [[Yeah! That's the idea.]]

MEDO_206 [[Oh, and when you want to speak out of character, we like to use these double brackets to make it obvious.]]

I wasn't exactly an unpopular kid, I had friends. I played soccer and rode my bike and collected *Magic: The Gathering* cards and slammed POGs and got good grades and had sleepovers and kissed girls and read *Animorphs* and whatnot.

I seemed well suited to the world outside my home.

It's just that the world outside the home is *such* a different place, and you learn to adapt to it. The sterile drabness of the highschool hallways, the idle chit-chat and politics of preteens and not-quite-ready-for-college students. The sun-drenched desert of the beach that blisters your feet and carries the scent of sunscreen in the wind. The practiced hustling of buskers and carnival game shouters, the neon glow and incessant electronic noise pollution of arcade machines promising delights at 11 at night while people crammed popcorn and pizza and funnel cake at the firework-bookended finale of their family's vacation to the South Jersey boardwalk.

"You gonna eat with us or just sit at your computer all night again?" Mom called out.

The world inside my home was different. It carried the uniquely inescapable scent of family.

Dinnertime. Pizza. I grabbed a big greasy slice of pepperoni and threw it on a paper plate, then heel-turned my way back to my bedroom. Using money I earned from my summer job at the boardwalk arcade, I bought myself a new computer for my 15th birthday. I had the slice half in my mouth as I booted up WinMX again.

"Mo fankfh, Mom. M'buvy."

***

NightWanderer_305 [[Hey guys!]]

Kaska_484 [[Alright, where did we leave off?]]

MEDO_206 [[You just defeated the goblins. We found a pile of treasure and were gonna wait until today to go through it.]]

NightWanderer_305 *Arkemis digs through the gold, laughing his head off.*

Kaska_484 *Keeva is still going through the goblin corpses.*

NightWanderer_305 Whoa, look at this! *He holds up a shiny belt. It's covered with jewels.*

MEDO_206 [[Oh man can I recommend something crazy?? >_>]]

NightWanderer_305 [[Yeah?]]

MEDO_206 [[Put it on, and let me narrate]]

NightWanderer_305 [[Okay...?]]

NightWanderer_305 *Arkemis puts on the belt. Fits like a glove!*

MEDO_206 *Arkemis suddenly feels a little strange. He's shrinking!*

Kaska_484 O_o

NightWanderer_305 [[What the fuck? O_O]]

MEDO_206 [[Just wait, just wait]]

NightWanderer_305 Ahhh! I'm shrinking!???

MEDO_206 *Arkemis notices that his hair is growing out, and two boobs push out of his chest*

Kaska_484 [[Medo what are you doing to the guy? <_<]]

MEDO_206 *Arkemis has turned into a girl version of himself!!!*

MEDO_206 Oh no, Arkemis! That's the Girdle of Masculinity/Femininity! It changed you into a girl!

NightWanderer_305 [[I'm going to kill you. ><]]

NightWanderer_305 I... oh no. *Arkemis looks at his... boobs?*

Kaska_484 [[hahahahahahahahahahahahaha XDD]]

MEDO_206 [[XD we can retcon that if you want. It was stupid.]]

NightWanderer_305 [[Yes please.]]

***

My eyes refocus as I wake up from my screen-locked stare. I look away from the computer, processing that the room had been here the whole time I was gone. It's watching me, waiting for me to react. The text on the monitor keeps scrolling, but I am no longer inside it. My friends and the adventure eventually disappear into the jumble of color like it always does. I register that my parents are still in the kitchen, eating pizza and laughing like drunken idiots. My little sister has her door closed and locked.

That was ridiculous.

I look at my hands. I like the idea of a gender changing belt, but I don't know what to do with the feeling. How do you even roleplay that? It's a stupid fantasy to think about a belt turning anyone into a girl.

Wow, I love having such big boobs!
I love boys and clothes and makeup and shopping!
So stupid.

Frustrated, I close and lock the door, pull some tissues, spit into my hand, and masturbate.

***

You could be whoever you wanted to be in these chat rooms. You could even change your name whenever you wanted. I considered the username field and wondered what other potential it had. We often changed our names to suit the characters we were using to tell our stories. I was **NightWanderer_305** or **Anvil_305** or **Derrick_305** or whatever the situation called for.

I always personally used the number 305 in my username to signal to friends that it was me and not some random nobody in the crowd. That was how we protected ourselves from the scroll. It set us apart from the other strangers in the chat forums we frequented. It was my personal brand, my protection against anonymity.

I wanted to be known, right? I wanted people to see me as I am. As me, as the normal boy from the little beach town where no one lives all the time.

Outside, I could hear the distant rumbling booms of thunder clouds gathering over the Atlantic. The mood shifted as the temperature outside dropped and the wind changed. It sounded like it might be a big storm coming.

Why would they give me the ability to change my username if they didn't want me to? This username field was only a tool, a means of expression, a creative outlet. And it was sitting *right there* for me to pick up and use.

What if I just... pretended to be a girl?

It would be harmless, right? No one would know.

That would be pretty funny. Like a joke.

Kayla Hey everyone, what's up?

[[NEW YOU PROCESSING CHAMBER]]

TAGS: TG, MENTAL CHANGES, TECHNOLOGY, MAGICAL, UNWILLING, TRICKED

In the year 2055, some cities installed special machines in various places that would allow you to change your appearance or personality. However, they weren't perfect, and as a result some pranksters took advantage of loose restrictions to trick their friends.

One day, David was shoved into a prepaid machine by his so-called friends, and the doors locked behind him.

"Have fun in there!" They laughed.

"Let me out! This isn't funny!" David pounded on the door. The selection screen came on behind him.

<Welcome to the New You Processing Chamber. Please be advised that you will only be able to leave the chamber once the process has completed and it is safe to do so. Please answer the following questions, and we will get started.>

1. Are you straight, gay, bisexual, asexual, or other?

David scoffed and selected **[STRAIGHT]**. "Can't believe they put me in here. Maybe I can get out without too many changes if the selections are close enough to who I am now."

2. Hair color? [BROWN]

3. Eye color? [HAZEL]

These selections went on and on, with Dave choosing the options that were closest to his real self. He hadn't noticed any real changes yet.

17. Please enter your body type. [ATHLETIC]

Finally, an option that could be an improvement on his current self and not have him feel too bad.

Upon selecting this option, he started to feel an actual change in his body. His body fat melted away like it was nothing. He felt much better.

18. What kind of girl are you?

Dav paused on this selection in disbelief. "Wait, what kind of *girl*?? This is a girl's booth they threw me in!? Holy shit, guys, let me out now!" Dav pounded on the door and frantically tried to open the locked latch.

<If no selection is made, one will be chosen for you.>

Freaking out, Da reviewed the options, and regrettably chose the option that seemed to be the least intrusive to his personality.

18. What kind of girl are you? [COOL]

D felt a little different. Like... they were above it all. Above this stupid machine. They were confident they'd be able to reverse it in the end, and they didn't give a shit about the guys outside, even though they could hear they were still laughing.

19. Choose a hairstyle. [LONG, BANGS]

D was confident they'd reverse the whole thing, so they decided it didn't matter what they chose for the rest of this program.

Their now longer hair was neat and styled, they had a remarkably pretty face, and they sported two generously sized breasts after choosing their cup size. They even ended up with an above-average sensitivity in their new vagina. Their transformation into a girl was more or less complete.

31. What role do you play during sex? [BOTTOM]

Well that one's easy.

32. How do you like your men? [DOMINANT]

Whatever.

9,G{sM2 didn't even realize that she wasn't into women anymore. After all the button pressing and such, she hadn't put it together that her first selection of "Straight" happened to be from the woman's perspective. B(@y8$ liked men, that much was so obvious to her. She even chose some of the more delicious sex positions that she enjoyed the most.

39. Do you like being a woman? [NO]

There it was! The option that would surely change her back into a man. S+8=GbJ casually selected "no" and leaned back smiling.

The machine paused and whirred and clicked.

<We are sorry to hear this. New You has a 100% Satisfaction Guarantee. We promise, you'll love being a woman again when you exit this chamber.>

!x'X"4z blinked, and the panic returned. "No, that's not what I want. That's not what I want! Let me out!"

The colors spiraled and changed inside the chamber, and *WxE'2;>* felt herself relax. She had nothing to worry about, she was a sexy woman with a great libido and tons of hot guys waiting outside for her. She loved being a woman, after all.

40. Thanks for using New You. One final question: What is your name?

The girl instinctively knew what to enter, so she traced the buttons on the console with her freshly manicured fingers.

[KAYLA]

The machine's colors died down and the lock clicked. A drawer slipped open to reveal the clothing and purse that she had selected. Kayla got changed, and then–satisfied with the changes–strolled outside with confidence.

She glanced at the men gawking at her. "Hey boys, which of you wanted to get lucky tonight?"

II

LIAR

TAGS: KAYLA, THE AUTHOR, FAMILY

ghost_827 How are you, Kayla?

Kayla didn't exist. To be asked a question so directly was an event so catastrophic that the formless void around her shook and tore and exploded into form. The empty black became black. The space where she was positioned now had coordinates, definition. Had she possessed muscles enough to receive and filter and expel air, she could have moved what could be considered lips to speak an answer in response. This disastrous question called on her to react in kind, to provide justification and meaning for her non-existence in her own words.

It gave her life.

Kayla I'm fine. :)

The motion blur of letters and words and colors in the window was overwhelming. Tangled lines of discussion wove like fabric and created a tapestry. After recovering from the suddenness of being brought forth into existence, she realized that no one else had talked to her since that first time. It seemed like the dialogue would move on without her if she didn't keep up. Just as soon as she had been brought to stand before these words, she felt herself fading back into the obscurity of nothing. This fabric was woven by many voices, and Kayla only held one thread.

It felt good to exist. That was a feeling she wanted again. And if she could receive existence by the acknowledgement of one voice, she imagined how good it might feel to receive it from many.

Emboldened, she rang out into the black. "How is everyone?" And the voices would ring back in fireworks of warmth and welcome every time.

She discovered that she could recreate her existence in this way whenever she wanted. These voices didn't know she didn't exist. They didn't care. They never questioned the game she played to feed the hunger to keep herself from fading back to that emptiness.

Kayla hunted and gathered for sustenance in the presence of these shapeless voices. She was addicted to this life, insofar as she needed to cling to it for her survival.

***

I'm a liar. I was taking advantage of these people's trust by giving them the wrong information. I kept telling them I'm a girl named Kayla when truly I was—

It doesn't matter. Dad got home, and he stumbled into my room for some reason. He didn't need to get close for his stench to wash over me. His clothes smelled like ash and booze. He had a rough day. I kicked myself for leaving the door open.

"Whas haaappenin'?" he chuckled, leaning against my door frame. He was completely gone. With shaky hands I clicked the mouse to close the program on the computer, and turned to face him. His eyes drooped.

"Didja have a gooday, son?" I didn't know why he was here. Maybe he was lost? Maybe he genuinely cared about my answer. Maybe the good parent hidden deep inside his brain was fighting against whatever monster kept driving him to the bar, a decent man wanting to express concern for the happiness of his children.

I wanted him to go away.

"I'm fine, Dad."

"Whaddya up to?"

My chest tightened. "Nothing, just doing some homework." I'm a liar.

His lips turned up as his brain registered the correct sequence to form a smile. "Mm. Thas good. Heyyy, you wan pizza tonight?"

I turned back to the computer, mostly because it was hard to look him in his drifting eyes. If I stopped paying attention to him, maybe he'd disappear.

"Yeah, sounds good. Thanks."

***

ghost_1495 What are you up to, Kayla?

The words pulled her back. The exciting tingle of consciousness returned with the light, and she had a sense of self again. She would float from room to room like this, disappearing in one place and

28

reappearing in another. She'd reach out to all the strange voices in these places in a bid for her life and reincarnate every time.

Kayla Nothing. Just homework.

She wanted to know these voices. But mostly, she wanted the voices to help her get to know herself.

ghost_62915 Cool. Homework sucks.

She was trapped. And she knew that she could vanish at any moment. She'd exit the world and be consumed by the black, only to reappear some arbitrary time later. She had no real control over her presence, and so she struggled to hold tight to the words that allowed her to feel whole in the moment.

This went on for a little while—not that time had any meaning to Kayla. As far as she knew, time was a concept that only applied to people who existed. She didn't age; in fact, she held a special power to define herself in whichever way she wanted to. And if it ever mattered to the voices that gave her life, she'd choose whichever age felt the most comfortable for them.

Kayla was incapable of lying. She recognized that she was an entity where truth was meaningless. She fed on this whenever she could.

The words flicker and are extinguished, as they always are. The black crawls around her and suffocates her existence.

***

I'm startled as the door opened. Dad shouted at me.

"Couldn't you hear me? Pizza's here! Come on!"

Annoyed, I was left with a feeling of whiplash. Maybe I'd have an easier time chatting without interruption later at night. I felt bad for leaving the conversation so abruptly, but I reminded myself it doesn't matter.

No one would care if she disappeared.

Kayla's fake anyway.

GULLS

TAGS: THE AUTHOR, WILLING, SEAGULLS

Laughing gulls aren't the kind of company to keep if you're trying to develop self-confidence. They're a common South Jersey seagull with a black head and neck, a crisp white belly, and a slate gray back with black-tipped wings. Their eyes are like clown eyes. They're all over the place.

They cackle constantly.

HA HA HA HA HA HA HA HA HA HA HA HA HA

I mean, they're bullies, right? They watch your every move, laugh without regard for your feelings, and steal your lunch when you're not looking. One time, a gull stole a slice of pizza right out of my hands. Another pooped in my friend's hair.

They didn't know any better, and that kind of gave them some charm. I once entertained a flock of these stupid birds, laughing and jittering and cawing and stumbling over each other as they fought over a french fry I had tied to a string. I'd yank it away from them right as they got close enough to try to grab it.

So stupid.

As a teenager, I took my first job in a small boardwalk arcade by the beach. I cleaned and repaired crane machines, slot machines, and other such gambling devices for super. I vacuumed. I learned how to be charismatic for strangers and snuck Tootsie Rolls from the prize showcases. I was paid in wads of dollar bills, packed tightly into a white envelope with my name written on it in pencil. I worked there for six hot summers.

***

It's the beginning of the summer.

"Your hair is kind of gross, why is it so long?" Vanessa, my boss's cute daughter, asked me.

I hadn't put much thought into it. I guess it was getting a little long. I thought it was kind of a cool skater look. Maybe I wasn't showering as much as I needed to?

"My sister and I have been wondering... are you *gay*?" She leaned so hard on that last word, it buckled under her weight.

"No! I'm not gay!" The words leapt out of my mouth faster than I registered that I was speaking them.

"Well, I haven't seen you go out with any girls since I've known you."

"I like girls." I liked Vanessa.

[[I liked her effortless sense of style.]]

"I've had girlfriends." This was a partial truth, if you count the kind of innocent awkward professions of love that happen in classrooms in the seventh grade.

She raised an eyebrow at my outfit, and I realized that she was judging me. I wasn't particularly organized or well put together: a flowery Hawaiian button up shirt with some dragons on it, and ratty jeans *well* past their expiry date. The fabric was loose and thin on my shoes.

It's not like I had much money. My parents never gave me any money, which was why I took this job in the first place. Clothing ended up being the last thing on my list to prioritize buying for myself.

I didn't want to be gay. Wasn't that a bad thing? I knew one gay kid at school, but everyone said they were weird, and I didn't want to be weird. My father called them a faggot. And besides, I wanted girlfriends. I wanted to be around more girls.

"We should take you shopping!" She said, her eyes wide and beaming.

I hated shopping. Shopping was something adults did for Christmas and birthdays. I knew when to expect my annual clothing update, and it was always black or gray or otherwise boring clothes delivered to me in a much more colorfully wrapped box. Clothes shopping was for girls, anyway. They were the ones who had choice and color and style.

I found myself in a skate shop by the beach that sold trendy clothes for boys. Vanessa took me under her wing and showed me all the fashionable options. She picked out shirts and hoodies for me to wear. New pants that fit wide around the legs. A baseball cap. New sneakers, in black and gray. I don't remember enough details about what they picked out. It all blended together. I bought it all with my hard-earned arcade money and walked out of there a new man.

The laughing gulls continued their harassments from overhead.

HA HA HA HA HA HA HA HA HA HA HA HA HA

It's the middle of the summer.

Vanessa, not yet done with her quest to fix me, went with me to the local barbershop. There was something about going to a barbershop without my parents around and getting to make a choice like this for myself. The bearded barber had an average man's haircut. It looked like all the other men's hair in town. With Vanessa there to cheer me on, the man shampooed and washed my greasy hair, cleansing me of all my misgivings that brought me here with a head of hair worth getting upset about.

The lifeless faces of extremely beautiful women stared at me from the plastered walls. These posters hadn't been changed out in years, and half of them were sun-faded. But look! They showed *all* the ways women get their hair styled and primped and preened and tousled and shaped and decorated and put up and put down.

God, it must have been exhausting to be an attractive woman and have so many choices on how you want to appear to the world.

I resented the many girl faces on the wall judging me for my comparative laziness. The only man face on the wall looked exactly like the guy giving me the haircut, and he didn't seem at all interested in what was going on.

The barber gave me an average man's haircut. I got my nearly-shoulder-length hair buzzed down. I'd been growing that hair for over a year, but it's not like I knew what to do with long hair. Nobody ever taught me anything or expressed interest in it other than Vanessa, who wanted to get rid of it.

"Wow!" Vanessa beamed. "That looks so much better!"

I stared at my reflection. I would never grow it out again. At least she wouldn't think I was gay now.

The dinned soundtrack of the birds was still playing outside. Undoubtedly, they had followed me here, too.

HA HA HA HA HA HA HA HA HA HA HA HA HA

It's the end of the summer.

The endless kaleidoscope of umbrellas dotting the beach landscape has dwindled down to a scant few as the summer heat has faded and many of the boardwalk attractions and copycat t-shirt and souvenir shops have closed.

The arcades are still open though, and I have the day off.

Since I had the keys to the machine, I could play practice games of *Dance Dance Revolution* on a professional gaming cabinet as often as I wanted to. I got pretty good at it, and at this point I was feeling like I was finally ready to try to beat *Era* by TaQ on the Heavy-difficulty setting. My friends said they'd join me at the Gateway 26 arcade, which had the best machine on the boardwalk. It sat under an awning to protect the screen from too much glare, and it faced out to the beach so tourists walking by could enjoy the show as a scrawny teenager chased after colorful arrows to the rhythm of *Butterfly* and *Captain Jack*.

It was a fun hobby! And look, I'm doing well.

My heart rate is up, my blood is pumping.

And seven older boys showed up in a group behind me to watch.

And heckle.

And one guy got on the pad next to me.

And mocked my determined dancing as the others laughed.

And called me a faggot.

And I tried to ignore them hoping they'd get their laughs in and leave.

And the song was almost over anyway.

And then I felt a leg take a sweep at my leg.

And I stumbled.

And I turned and brought my leg swiftly up to connect with the guy's nuts.

And it wasn't enough.

And I was grabbed by the collar by a much stronger teenager.

And I was pulled to the center of the boardwalk where tourists walking by could enjoy the show as a scrawny teenager was circled by seven older guys and punched twenty times on the side of the face.

HA HA HA HA HA HA HA HA HA HA HA HA HA

The world around me gradually bent itself back into a shape I recognized. My ears were ringing and my whole body was numb. My head hurt. A different man, much older, stood over me as the music from the arcade started returning to focus.

He asked, "Why didn't you fight back?"

BUDDIES

The darkness was no comfort for Kayla, but it was enough to get by. She was a dream, a peripheral vision of an unknown master that called on her when they wanted to. Kayla learned contentment with her incorporeality and drew sustaining fruit of her non-life's meaning from each brief encounter with the strange voices of the WinMX chat room.

It was her place. This was where she adapted to the fraying and constant bleed of information about stranger's lives. They filled her cup and nurtured her sense of self by simply existing. She had no other options available.

These were the voices that gave her validation by simply addressing her directly.

Ghost_1820 Hey Kayla, I missed you.

Ghost_91832 Kayla, you're so funny!

Ghost_288 Kayla, where have you been?

These were her friends, they knew her in the only way they were able to.

37

Friends?

In the dark hours, Kayla's non-eyes opened into a username creation window, her tingle of consciousness awakening the same as before. But this felt different.

She had two feet now, which were planted firmly on what she could consider solid ground. She lacked the denseness of physicality, but she felt established with the pressure of a floor beneath her to support her. Gone was the wispiness of floating in a void as a thought, as a series of text messages in the shape of a girl exchanged only to be addressed as one. While she had no form, she gained a new awareness: perhaps one day, she could.

Look around.

On one side of her endless expanse she could see the colorful scrolling threads of the chat room.

On the other side, she noticed a new orange faceless thing in the shape of a blocky person. It looked like it was stuck in some kind of running pose. They looked friendly and inviting, but didn't say anything to her. A bright neon sign hovered above them. It read **Buddies (0/0).**

This was a gift, she surmised. With Buddies, she might be able to exist, and grow beyond her prison of words.

She wasted no time. She floated off to the fabric, her feet lifting off the ground. She knew she didn't have any permanence in this chaotic place, but she could bring friends to the place where she did.

Kayla Do you want to add me on AIM?

KillaFungus_322 sure!

A funny thing happened when she got her first Buddy. The instant the neon sign changed to **Buddies (1/1)**, Kayla went from "Nothing to Anyone" to "Something to Someone." This Buddy had an impression of her, a thought that lived somewhere within a person that actually existed. Kayla had been talking about how much she liked *Sailor Moon*, and about the episode she watched recently; therefore, to this Buddy, Kayla must be the kind of person who talks about shows she likes. She had gained the ability to define new character traits for herself.

This gave her form. At least for this Buddy, she was "Interested in Shows."

She never had character traits she could define for herself before—certainly not fixed ones. But now whenever she talked to **Killa-Fungus322**, she knew she had a few things that would always be true. She was a girl, she liked talking about TV, and she *existed*.

She felt joy building as warmth in her non-chest. She liked this discovery. She found many more Buddies, and they came from all sorts of places: anime chat rooms, roleplay servers, music lovers, skateboarders, scientists, politicians, adults only (18+), cat lovers, dog lovers, videogamers. She was a ghost capable of milking the Grand Central Station of the Internet. People coming in, passing through, talking about everything and nothing. She navigated the web to beg, borrow, and steal scraps of the world, and built an armor of humanity for herself.

> **James007** Are you really a girl?
>
> **Kayla** Yeah!
>
> **James007** Where are you from?

Kayla New Jersey, you?

James007 California, too bad! Hmmm, but are you cute? Haha.

Cute?

Kayla thought about this. Until now, she hadn't considered what she looked like. She'd never looked like anything before. But knowing what she knew about people, and how she was going to get more Buddies to cultivate an existence, she figured this would be a good opportunity.

Kayla I like to think so.

And so, her Buddy List grew and grew. She looked upon her empire of Buddies as a container of her character. It was everyone she knew, and everything she knew that was true about herself. The once formless dream had dimensions now. The faceless orange person looked on with approval.

Buddies (82/123)

Kayla existed on the Internet as a person who could be found.

III

41

BLUEBERRIES

TAGS: THE AUTHOR, FAMILY, UNWILLING, ALCOHOL

"Hey man, where's your beer?"

A stocky guy wearing a Mets baseball cap and an Eagles jersey shouted to me over the music and chatter at a party at a friend of a friend's campus apartment, bringing me into the present.

I stood against a wall that hadn't been cleaned in years. The place was super crowded, filled with red cups and cans and bottles of whatever in the hands of young college hopefuls. I didn't do parties like this; they always felt uncomfortable. But I knew I couldn't stay away from these things forever. Besides, I didn't come alone.

"Oh, I don't drink." I shouted back.

"What? Like, never? That sounds super fucking corny, dude," He laughed. "Why don't you drink?"

His drunken chuckle triggered my adrenaline response. Visions of nights passing by slowly as I waited for my parents to take me home. Intoxicated jaws hung agape, large meaty hands the size of my skull ruffled my hair and thanked me for being patient as they poisoned themselves. The stochastic laughter of many in the crowded bar. The wretched stink of booze on clothes and skin and hair. Eyes closed, sweaty palms in the air. Cups or mugs or glasses or shots loosely gripped as sticky foamy ichor dripped down arms and spilled on the floor as the shadows of adults danced to the same music as the weekend before. How can anyone be enjoying this?

Everyone here was killing themselves.

***

I don't drink alcohol. I never have, save for the one time Dad had me try a foamy sip from his frosty Budweiser can when I was nine. The scrape of cold metal on my teeth was chased by squelch on my tongue. I made a face, and spat.

I grew up in a house of smoke and laughter. I recall the smell. The cabinets were lined with many labeled bottles and cans, and my father's breath was strong with it. Our carpet smelled of dog and cat urine that was rarely cleaned, and the haze of cigarette smoke hung like a curtain in every hallway.

My parents would frequently take my little sister and I to their favorite local bar. Every day, almost. What's a single day for a child? A lifetime? They'd bring us in, and we would meet their friends and their friends would say how much bigger we had gotten since the last time they saw us. The bar was filled with as much smoke and as many clinking glasses and drunk men and women as our house usually contained, so we were used to it. This was the backstage scenery of our lives.

It was a place where everyone loved us, but no one paid attention to us. My sister and I would reach up to slide shuffleboard discs on the long wooden table and draw smiley faces in the grit with our fingers, while the adults sang country songs about drinking whiskey and having friends in low places. Our drunk parents would drive us home.

Dad beat Mom sometimes. He'd stumble around the house and his words wouldn't work and he'd sound like an idiot. I'd retreat to my room, to seek shelter from two rampaging beasts, and wait for them both to go to bed. Sometimes the two of them got into a bad fight and I'd hear a dull sound of fists impacting flesh. Two titans crashed through the house as my mother fought back. She was not a weak woman, either. And no one in the house was free from the call to violence. I'd smash my Lego and K-Nex creations into pieces against my dresser. My little sister punched holes in her wall, and would hide the damage beneath her *Yu Yu Hakusho* and *Naruto* wall scrolls.

It's not like there was one specific triggering moment where I decided "I'm never going to drink or smoke or do drugs." It was a fact. Like a line of default code that came prepackaged with my consciousness when it finally booted up and said, *"wake up, you're a person now."*

***

Quiet.

A child's quiet, a dreaminess recollected, not experienced with intention, present before true consciousness is called forward.

With the exception of the whistling of cold air coming off from the Atlantic, and the gentle breathing of two young children sleeping soundly under warm blankets. The boy is three. The baby girl has just turned one.

A glass door opens with a whine.

The inner door knob creaks and fidgets, but doesn't grant entrance.

A loud thud, wood fibers strain and buckle from the impact.

A louder thud, the sound amplified by a greater force acting upon the wooden door.

The door gives.

The toddler is startled by sudden shouting of demanding voices in his home. He wakes, already crying. His little sister is in her crib, crying as well.

A large man the boy doesn't recognize trudges into his bedroom and picks him up. He recognizes the man's uniform, neatly pressed dark blue with a badge and straps and a gun—a policeman. He's seen this man in picture books, parades and crosswalks. But what's a policeman doing here, in his bedroom, when he's trying to sleep? The boy is escorted out of his bedroom, still crying, with his sister carried close behind by another man. The men press on past the children's parents, who are both face-down, handcuffed on the stained and shaggy carpet.

The boy sees Mom's angry face. He sees another policeman kneeling on top of Dad. He sees the splintered door where the police forced their entry. Deep inside of his developing brain, an electrical spark ignites and forms a connection.

The children are escorted out of sight of their prone parents and left in the temporary care of their upstairs neighbor. The one who has that loud white cockatiel, the tarantula, and many different lizards and snakes in tanks. Her place smells like a zoo.

The boy's next time seeing his mother will be at a prison.

The next time Mom comes home, he'll be five.

The chaotic scene freezes around him like a painting blurred around the edges, and lodges itself firmly as his first memory.

***

I wanted nothing to do with their contamination. Alcoholism was a disease that you could catch if you weren't careful, and so I was very careful. I put myself on high alert whenever I saw alcohol at a party. In college I had to be extra vigilant because the parties were nonstop, and alcohol started appearing in places where I didn't expect it. I would hear the slurred words and the vile wetness of drunkenness of my father and mother on the tongues of my friends.

"Moonshine?" My jovial friend casually offered me a silver flask from his hip. My eyes would hold fast to the container of mystery liquid and register *danger*. I'd shake my head no, waving it off, and he'd shrug and say something like, "More for me, then," and kick his head back and take a swig with a satisfying, performative "*ahhh*."

After I'd told enough people that I didn't drink, the offers would mostly stop. Though people had this habit of being nice *just in case*, and often gave me the out to partake if I ever changed my mind. But whenever I met someone new, and the topic came up, I'd have to tell the same story over again.

"I don't drink."

"Why not?"

"I just don't."

Their eyes always regarded my story with some mix of curiosity, jealousy, shame. I imagined the questions racing through their heads.

How did this guy figure it out?

What, like they think they're better than me?

What's so wrong with drinking?
He can't even try a little bit?
How do they have fun?

Stumped, they'd shrug their shoulders and move on, and I'd be left to wonder when I'd have to explain my life's non-choices to someone again.

***

I'm allowed to have preferences, right? Certainly I'm entitled to likes and dislikes. That's what a personality is! And I know who I am. I'm me.

I go to a great school, and I'm going to be a great marketer. I have a girlfriend who's pretty and chill and makes me laugh a lot. I have a great job, and they like me there. I have great friends.

[[I jack off to sissy porn at night.]]

I eat sundaes *without* a cherry on top.

[[I pretend to be a girl to talk to guys online.]]

I don't do drugs.

I don't drink.

What am I supposed to say? "Sorry, I'm afraid that if I drink now, I might lose control and become just like my parents. Become just like you. Become just like everyone else."

I don't get tattoos. Dad has tattoos. They're not for me. I don't get piercings, because what's the point? Why should I do any of those things? I've come this far without doing anything like that, and I've turned out fine!

[[I don't know why I do these things.]]

I don't ride rollercoasters.

I don't drink milkshakes.

[[I don't know how to stop.]]

I wake up, I get dressed. I go to school or practice or work. I put on the show. I fit in my little box and perform. I get good grades. I have a brand. I'm me. I'm a two-dimensional caricature of myself. I've designed the person I am in my head and followed all the programming. Introducing any new element to this delicate balance of self-worth requires an inordinate amount of work and reflection. You can't expect me to change. I don't know who or what I am, but at least I know what I won't do.

I won't eat blueberries.

***

"Wait, what's wrong with blueberries?" My cousin Cody asked me.

The sun was out. I was sweaty after playing a game of tag around my grandfather's yard.

"Would you eat a bug?" I challenged him, sitting in the shade, poking at a group of ants with a blade of freshly mowed grass.

"Of course I would. Assuming I knew it was safe to eat, I'd eat anything."

I made a pouting face in disgust. "That's gross. I would never eat a bug."

"Well maybe you should try one sometime. There's chocolate-covered grasshoppers and edible silkworms and all kinds of stuff that people eat every day."

"Why?"

He smiled. "Why not? Would you really be willing to go your whole life without trying something like that? Would you go your whole life without eating a blueberry just because you decided that it was bad, somehow?"

***

I didn't question it. Alcohol was simply a *thing* that I had to deal with, and I got to witness how it was used to make Dad angry and violent, my mother mean and resentful. I heard stories of teenagers making bad decisions and hurting themselves and dying over the stuff. And for what?

If I don't become a person who needs alcohol, I won't need to drink it.

"So you think you're better than me, huh?" Mom said, her eyes half open. She stank of Jack Daniels, she loomed in the kitchen as a dreadful vision of a human.

"No, Mom, but I think that if you drank less—"

"Oh, so high and mighty!" She used my full name in an attempt to make it crystal clear her aggressions sat with *me*, so I couldn't be confused about her intention. "Thinks he's the golden child. The teenager that thinks he has it all figured out." I could taste the venom spouting from her lips, for she spat it at me with every *kuh* and *tuh* and *fff* and *sss* sound she made. "Fuck you."

The answer was really, really simple: *I wouldn't be like them.*

***

I'm brought back to the present by the stench of beer as it wafts past my face. Some idiots shambled down the hallway in the small shitty college apartment lined with the same edgy posters everyone had, and a girl who is definitely too young to drink turns and awkwardly apologizes for bumping into me before laughing and returning to her friends. I notice the guy in the Mets cap with a stupid look on his face is *still* waiting for me to tell him why I'm so super fucking corny.

I didn't drink. But I couldn't exactly get into the reasons with this asshole, could I? What happens to a person when they define their existence by things they don't do? When pickiness becomes a personality trait. Or a tool to maintain control in an otherwise chaotic life.

I'm going to get my life in order. I don't need this deviancy. I'm better than these people. I'm going to make it. I'm going to be a good person.

I decided the better response would be to simply ignore him. I shook my head and went to find my friend. I wanted to go home.

LABYRINTH

TAGS: KAYLA, WILLING

James007 Sooo, I was wondering. What do you look like? :)

Kayla was good at this, and she had gotten much better with her words now that she had practice. She came to understand what a girl looked like, and how to talk about being one. Rosy details bloomed from this experience to paint a picture of a beautiful liar.

> **Kayla** I'm a shorty. 5'1, and I have long red hair, and green eyes.
>
> **Kayla** My mom's like super Scottish.
>
> **James007** Sounds like you are pretty cute! :)
>
> **James007** I hope it's not too much to ask but I'd love to actually see you.
>
> **James007** Do you have a photo?

This question always reminded Kayla of her lack of personhood. She would make excuses like *Sorry, not comfortable sharing* to make an attempt to both keep her Buddy and answer the question fairly. If her Buddy didn't like her answer, she'd have to delete and block them, too. She already had to give up some Buddies this way.

But she liked James. He took an interest in her, asking her more questions to get to know her, and provided the largest canvas on which to paint. He was never pushy. She wanted to repay his kindness by gifting him someone to look at.

Unfortunately, Kayla wasn't "someone." Her Buddies certainly *considered* her to bear the resemblance of someone, but she came to understand that someones have faces and bodies and hearts and brains and blood and urine and age. She had none of those things.

She adapted, there were many places online where she could borrow a face—at least temporarily. There were cute faces, sweet faces, sexy faces, neutral faces, boring faces, ugly faces, happy faces, sad faces. Her resentment boiled, seeing all these faces on someones. Why wasn't *she* born with a face? And what did these people do to deserve theirs? What was their secret to having a face?

She scoured the endless expanse of faces and made notes. Short, beautiful, round, fat, light, skinny, ugly, brown, blue, heavy, hot, dark, graceful, powerful, gorgeous, tall, shy, beaming, red, tan, hazel, wide, proud. She compared and compared herself to these faces until she came across one that spoke to her with a kernel of relatability.

That one looks like me.

It wasn't perfect, Kayla knew that. For all the faces in the world, nothing could match exactly. She couldn't look in a mirror.

She would never look like anything.

This had to be good enough. It was a means to an end. Filled with resolve and a little guilt, she took the photo of some girl in Utah named Fiona and claimed it as her own.

Right click.

Save As.

Kayla This is me!

James007 Wow! You're gorgeous!

It was exhausting defining herself over and over again to her long list of Buddies. Sometimes Kayla felt short, red-headed, and Scottish, other days she felt tall, blonde, with big blue eyes. She would shapeshift to suit her wild mood, use the spare parts of online girls she found attractive, and create an amalgamation of a suitable self from among them. She wasn't just one girl with a single face, she was a collection, she had tipped herself into something of an unbounded monstrosity that always put the best face forward.

This landed her in trouble occasionally. The game got more complicated the more Buddies she had, as they remembered faces that she would forget. **KillaFungus322** thought she was a preppy brunette from New Jersey, but **SparkleDemon96** thought she was a raven-haired tattooed goth chick from Chicago. These contradictions meant nothing to Kayla, but they meant everything to her Buddies.

Kayla Yeah, growing up in California will do that to you hahaha

KillaFungus322 Hold up, I thought you said you were from New Jersey?

Kayla Oh, sorry, uh...

Block.

Delete Buddy.

Shit. What a mess.

Shamed, she looked up to the neon sign above her blocky orange friend and lamented it dropping a single number. She couldn't keep losing Buddies like this, they were the only things keeping her from unraveling into that dark non-existence again. She couldn't go back to that place. She couldn't afford to let go. She needed protection.

The silence surrounding her gave way to a low bass humming. It might've been mistaken for adrenaline: the way the vibrations of distant sounds settle into a body, bringing hair follicles to life on skin. Far beyond what could be measured in units for a space that has no shape or size, thunderclouds began to make their presence known.

Kayla leaned into these jitters. She resolved to get organized. Get a better memory.

I can do this myself.

She started by logging details about her appearance into a simple Notepad file with "Kayla" scrawled in the header. It was everything she shared: every specific conversation she'd had with her Buddies, a catalog of all the little intricacies of her hydra of a contradictory existence, a tool to keep her story straight. Every name she'd ever used, every height, every birthday, every place she lived. What once were words as wind passing over the Earth now became chiseled into rock and settled into permanence.

She held and admired this thing she made. This thing that was fully and uniquely hers. It had a vulnerable glow to it, casting candlelight and warmth she could cup in her non-hands. This little Notepad file was Kayla's soul.

I'll protect you.

Right click. Create New Folder.
Right click. Create New Folder.
Right click. Create New Folder.

The endless dark void around her was disrupted as the empty ground beneath her feet quaked. Kayla curled her soul in her non-arms to shield it with her non-body, and braced against her faceless orange friend. The floor cracked and split into large sections that stretched beyond her vision. From the depths of nowhere, enormous vanilla-colored folder icons burst from the crevices and erected tall walls around her. They nestled inside and around each other, creating a complex web of numbered and strangely named containers of information.

They branched and weaved and wandered, spreading out in all directions to the horizon. They cast an iron shadow. An impenetrable fortress.

Kayla coughed with her non-lungs as the dust settled. Her new space was still large but no longer unbounded, surrounded on five sides by the folders that loomed over her and her belongings. On the far wall was a door that opened to the voices of WinMX. In another corner her faceless orange friend stood resolute as a guard to her Buddy List, now affixed to the wall.

Against yet another wall stood a large and sturdy dresser with many, many doors. She opened one to find her collection of faces there. They smiled back at her, frozen still as the day she captured them.

Yes! This is good.

Emboldened by her self-creation, she turned to face the middle of the room. A gesture and a thought was enough to fashion herself a throne. It was trimmed with gold, with rich pink and red fabrics adorning the seat. An artisan's work befitting her station as royalty. She constructed a smaller structure, with a small pillow sitting atop of it. She let out a relaxed breath, and rested her soul on the cushion. She ran her non-fingers along the textures of her creation, and lowered herself down into the chair. Kayla took her place as Queen on her labyrinthian throne, resting comfortably in C://Desktop/Photos/boring/docs/a/x/f/963/donotuse/2915.

LEAVE

TAGS: MOM, DAD, POP-POP, THE HOUSE, CODY

"People who never leave, never change."

My parents had a hard time leaving, and I resented them for their weaknesses. I was never going to be like them.

MOM

Over the cacophony of drunken cheering and live rock music, in the attic of a cigarette smoke-filled fisherman's bar in a small corner of the map in the lower end of New Jersey, a newborn baby was heard crying—having only just started her life, born onto the splintery wooden floors and cropped from the umbilical cord attached to her mother.

Rough start.

Rushed to the hospital, she and her mother were healthy and fine. The baby was gently placed into the hands of a nice middle-class white married Protestant couple for $150.

Mom was told that her birth mother had fled a life in the Pine Ridge Oglala Lakota Native American Reservation some time ago to

57

find prosperity and happiness elsewhere. That she found a man who abused, impregnated, and left her with nothing multiple times.

That $150 was enough.

Mom's adoptive parents were mild-mannered and stern, and had a lovely home in a quiet neighborhood. They had a large yard with an unfenced tree line that went deep into the forested wilderness behind the house. Their neighbors were all well-off with families of their own. They went to church every Sunday.

She loved animals. With all the yard space, she cared for the forest critters she rescued: mending bird wings, creating safe encasements for all manner of reptiles, rabbits, and bugs, and one local skunk who had been attacked by a dog.

It was a good life on paper.

Mom came to understand early that she had been adopted, bought and sold, a child born on splintered wood. As she grew older, she found ways to cope. She took an interest in the art of Oglala Lakota culture—a culture in which she had no upbringing. She braided her hair, she hung posters with indigenous symbols on her wall and wore tie-dye shirts with howling wolves on them. She dangled dreamcatchers above her bed to repel nightmares.

The house was *supposed* to be safe. She was *supposed* to be protected by her family. Instead...

She dreamt of the life she should have had.

How much further could she get away?

She found drugs. The hard stuff. The kind you take when you want to leave behind the pressure, to escape captivity under the specter of religion. The one she was told to pray to, the one that allowed her to be taken away from her birth parents. The one that allowed for her abuse as a child. She rebelled, she was kicked out of high school, she hitchhiked around the country spending nights under stars in a tent on the side of the highway. She took the roads as far as the Pine Ridge Reservation in South Dakota to locate her birth mother. The woman, her mother, a stranger, was discovered sitting at a small local bar.

What are you doing here? There's nothing for you here. I don't want to talk to you.

Mom returned to her South Jersey home empty-handed, other than an angered thirst for rebellion.

One night, she found herself at a party where another girl was killed.

She found herself driving away from the scene with the dead girl's car.

She found herself sent away to a maximum-security women's prison for the next seven years.

She was 19.

DAD

Dad grew up in Philadelphia under the shadow of his father, who I knew as Pop-Pop. Pop-Pop was a devout Jehovah's Witness and a fully wholesome man. He did not take liquor, and he did not celebrate birthdays. He built his electrical contracting company in the family name and became a well-respected man in all the places he did his business.

He also whipped Dad with a belt.

Pop-Pop would appear to the job in a clean white van full of organized supplies and tools, and wore a crisp, pressed suit. He was always on time, formal and professional, and got the job done with care and attention to detail.

When Dad was finally old enough, Pop-Pop took him to learn the trade. He hated this. For as much as Pop-Pop was sober, Dad was the opposite. As clean and put together as Pop-Pop was, Dad was the opposite. His hair was a messy unbrushed mass of blonde. He joined a gang of rough-housing bikers looking to escape their life, to carve their names in the towns and streets they visited. He traveled around the Tri-state on his Harley and earned himself arrests and fines and situations that Pop-Pop fixed him out of.

Life came fast for Dad, he was always looking for an opportunity to get away.

Mom

Mom kept a sketchbook in prison. She drew what she knew. She drew the people and places she grew up with. She drew animals, horses, birds, snakes, skunks, rabbits. Having gone to prison so young, she didn't have a lot of other experiences to draw from.

When she finally got out, she was prepared to live. She returned to her hometown and reunited with the only man who cared enough to stay in contact. He was wild and blonde and untamable, a man with a Harley. He got her pregnant barely a month after she'd left prison.

The child born on splintered wood set up a tent and sat out front of an abortion clinic for three long nights. She watched as the women came in and out of that place with or without children.

She dreamt of the life she should have had.

And so, in the same small hospital in the same tiny speck on the map she grew up in, Mom gave birth to a son.

She named him after the small South Dakotan town her mother was from.

POP-POP

With his hard-earned money and the best intentions, Pop-Pop supported the purchase of two neighboring houses in the quiet part of the South Jersey beach town—one for him and his wife, and the other for Mom and Dad. Perhaps he did this because he was excited about being a grandfather. Perhaps it was to keep an eye on his son.

THE HOUSE

"I have a son, I have a son!" The blonde and thickly-mustached man called out through the halls of the hospital. He carried me, a fragile creature in his arms, holding my naked baby body up in the air to share his joy with alarmed staff.

And so it came to pass that Mom, having been out of prison for less than a year, found herself with a partner and a newborn. She was thrust into that next checklist of her life—parenthood.

Mom had no income, but was reassured by my Dad's enthusiasm for the journey ahead. They could escape their demons by focusing on this new project. With a little help from their parents they moved into a comfortable house with a welcoming wooden door. A beautiful two-story yellow stucco house that was walking distance to the beach. It was spacious and clean, with enough bedrooms for a big family, modern 1980s amenities, and a big fireplace. They got a gorgeous golden dog to share the space.

Ah, the house: the cozy protective bubble of safety and warmth. The house is where you become human. Where a concept becomes a person, becomes a parent or a child or a spouse or a roommate. When a person has connection to another person and begins to exist. Only people who exist have houses.

Mom wanted to exist, and she had her family, so perhaps now she could become human. After those years in prison, it was good to find the comforts of a house where she could escape the trappings of her old life. She adorned its walls with dreamcatchers and paintings of howling wolves.

Houses reflect back on those that live in them. Bottles and cans piled up on the countertop. The stench of cannabis and cigarette smoke clung to the fibers in the carpet and the paint chips on the wall. Particles expelled by sloppy mouths grew dewy and seeped into the wood. Unemptied garbage bins and ashtrays littered the floors and end-tables, and untreated stains on mirrors and porcelain left impressionistic paintings that revealed the nature of its tenants.

A house does not want. It does not want to care for itself. It does not want to care for the people in it.

The father did not want to care for the child, either.

The comforts of the house were not enough for Dad, who turned back to his escapism, his booze and cocaine. He consumed his income through his mouth and skin, which left little to nothing to provide support for the woman and child that shared his house.

Mom was left with few options to care for herself and her infant.

But she was clever, and she had connections. She made contact with a friend who had access to cocaine and worked out a deal where she could access his supply for distribution. It was easy to sell a product when you had a keen buyer living in the same house.

The house did not judge its tenants as it rotted from the inside. The bright cheery yellow stucco exterior belied the desperate drug operation within its walls. The child did not judge its parents as long as it was diapered and fed. It was dressed in bright cheery outfits that carried the scents of its caregivers' environment.

As the mother's operation expanded, a second child was added to the mix. A baby girl this time. The house didn't care as the girl's bedroom was painted in bright pinks and yellows to cover up the stains from smoke. It did not care that the golden dog died, or that it was buried in the backyard next to the dead cats and the dead hamsters and the dead chinchillas. It did not care about the stashes of drugs piled up in a secret room in its basement. The mother's enterprise continued to expand to keep up with the costs of raising two small children with a drunk and absent father. Until one night, the house was raided by the police.

The welcoming wooden door was kicked in, the parents were handcuffed face down on shaggy carpet. The mother was sent away to prison for another two years for violating parole.

Her children stayed with their father in the house.

DAD

Dad took on his father's electrical contracting business when Pop-Pop was ready to retire, but everything was different. He was regularly late. His hair was unkempt, he wore ragged shirts with stains on them. His mustache was thick and greasy, and sometimes he was just plain drunk.

For everything Pop-Pop was, Dad was the opposite.

Wildwood is well known for its retro style and ritzy-glam beach view hotels, and the family electrical business was the once-reputable service that installed many of the major lighting work projects around the town. Giant neon signs with flashing lights conveyed a bright and cheery atmosphere that promised fun and excitement. It was the same kind of inviting shine that casinos in Las Vegas and Atlantic City have: the flame that draws the moth, the lure for wandering eyes to ignore the underlying mechanisms of the ringing machines and monsters and labor and toil and sadness that cobbled it all together.

Dad fell deeper into alcoholism and his work suffered for it. People stopped calling with jobs, and he sank even lower. Eventually he stopped that work entirely and sold the big white truck with the ladder and the wires and the bucket of nails his kids sat in when he drove them to odd jobs or school. For a time he tried his hands at being a firefighter. His struggles bled into his home life as he and Mom became increasingly cruel to each other.

CODY

My cousins Eric and Cody were like older brother figures to me, they lived next door much of the time with Pop-Pop. I would later come to understand that this was because they had their own complicated childhoods with parents who were also incapable of caring for themselves.

Cody stood out. He had an unusually fair complexion for someone that lived in a beach town and didn't care much for going out into the sun. His hair was tufty, a bleach white-blonde color. His eyes were pale blue. He also almost exclusively wore black clothing, and surrounded himself with 'vampire stuff.'

He wasn't goth: he was *gothic*. He could regularly be found wearing poofy white shirts that you only see in person at renaissance faires and pants made from simple black fabric that an old-timey tailor cobbled together. He looked like he may have fallen through a portal from another time and landed in a small residential neighborhood that could never appreciate or understand him.

After all, he was different, and differences weren't celebrated.

"Cody is so weird," Mom would say.

"He's a fag," Dad would say.

Cody represented a strong contrast to his half-brother Eric, who was incredibly tall, studious, a little brawny, and overall plain and well-mannered. Eric commanded attention simply as a matter of fact: he had the confidence of someone who understood the world around him and wanted to let you in on it. He was a scientist and chose his words intentionally. Everyone respected Eric.

The two got along very well; they were complementary. Cody taught us everything he knew about witchcraft and ancient Egyptian mythology, whereas Eric taught us fun science experiments and how to play *Magic: The Gathering*.

I heard about the car accident.

Cody had been driven off a cliff somewhere in Arizona while visiting a friend. The details were murky and not shared much with me, but he had been hospitalized, then he was fine, that he was getting better, and a few weeks later I found him planted in a recliner at Pop-Pop's place next door.

He didn't look better.

He had lupus.

I didn't understand lupus. All I knew was that Cody looked paler than usual, and his strength was sapped. He had to walk with a cane now.

Lupus is an auto-immune disease where your immune system attacks healthy cells and tissues by mistake. Some people seem to think it can develop in response to traumatic events, such as a car flying off a cliff with you inside of it.

Long story short, Cody's body didn't like him anymore.

DAD

As I got older, I didn't spend much time at home. I found distractions: work, or staying out late with friends, or going to the boardwalk. It was apparent that neither of my parents were happy. We were all getting older, anxious and irritable to get away, and Dad frequently shared that he was ready to move on.

"We're going to move to Florida, kids!" He proclaimed one day.

"What? Really?" We'd respond bright-eyed in wonder.

Time would pass. "We're moving to West Virginia!"

Nothing happened.

"We're going to move to Kansas! Really, it's happening!"

Nothing ever happened. We realized nothing would ever happen.

Dad was always looking for that big change. A way to get out of his rut and out from the shadow of his life. He was living in the house that was bought for him, with a family that materialized by accident. He had no handlebars to grip, his former job having been selected for him. He was grasping at relevance.

He spent so much money. He spent the money he had, as well as the money he took out of the mortgage in secret. He bought himself a new motorcycle even though he hadn't ridden in years. His health started to falter, and he gained a lot of weight. My parents subjected themselves and their children to hell together for years, before the kids could escape to college. Dad figured that sticking around meant he could claim his payday inheritance that would save him from this life whenever Pop-Pop finally died.

Cody

Cody moved into the unit in the upper portion of Pop-Pop's house. The little old lady that lived there before had passed away recently, and all her doilies and white ruffled curtains and ornate picture frames filled with pictures of her grandchildren were eventually replaced by a large sarcophagus coffee table, pitch black black-out curtains and the powerful scent of sandalwood incense. A friendly little black cat named Marius was the bouncer to this welcoming satanic night-club of a home.

"Why can't he be normal?"

"Cody's a loser."

"What is the deal with his clothing?"

"He thinks he's a fucking vampire."

At the very least, Cody was able to be there for Pop-Pop, who was getting on in years. In the end, they made for an interesting pair of housemates, the Jehovah's Witness and the goth. Everyone was waiting for Pop-Pop to die for his money. Everyone was waiting for Cody to die so he'd stop being so goddamn weird.

Then Pop-Pop died.

It broke out like this:
There had been a last-minute change to his will.
Half of his wealth went to his church.
His four grandchildren split everything else.
Mom and Dad were left with nothing.

Cody said he'd take care of Pop-Pop's house. Moving himself into the now available downstairs unit meant he no longer needed to climb the stairs every day—a task that was proving more challenging for him as his health got worse. That also meant more room for redecorating. The once simple decor of my grandfather's belongings gave way to Cody's darker palette preferences.

My father hated Cody for it all.

"Hey, don't be like your parents." Cody told us. "You've got to leave this town. You've got to see more things in order to change. People who never leave, never change."

The cruelty continued. As Cody's body waged a war with itself, he was subjected to the ongoing petty war with his family. There was no kindness shared with a person no one wanted to understand, someone who determined life's meaning for themselves, even as they were crumbling in front of everyone.

Cody grew weaker and more alone in the house. I had gone to college out-of-state, his brother was away at war. Cody's own parents left him to languish. He cocooned himself with his morbid fascinations and squeezed every ounce of joy from them.

At the age of 29, left to its own defenses, Cody's body did the last thing it could.

TOUCH

TAGS: KAYLA, WILLING

The cold steel floor was a great comfort, Kayla thought. She laid on her non-back, non-arms outstretched, soft brown non-hairs spreading every which way as it sprawled out. She wore a white sundress with cute green leaf patterns on it, sandals on her non-feet. Her non-eyes were covered by a pair of designer sunglasses, and a pinkish tint of gloss brightened her non-lips. She felt pretty. She felt like a girl.

This must be happiness.

Though, it was so quiet. Apart from the occasional pings coming from her Buddy List, she heard no other sound. The orange faceless friend was a silent sentry, hardly a companion at all. She wondered if anyone would ever visit. Her vision tracked up towards the peak of her maze walls. There was no way anyone would find her here.

All the same, it might be nice to be seen by someone. Or to talk to someone. Or to be touched.

Touched?

Kayla's non-face wrinkled up. She got it; she couldn't be touched. Even if someone did find their way to her, she had nothing to hold or feel. She kicked her non-self for thinking that she would ever stop wanting anything. It didn't hurt. She felt no pain.

That didn't seem fair.

What was the point of existing if you couldn't be seen or heard or touched or smelled? There was no one here to talk to or share things with. Even her Buddies could only see her non-face photos. They didn't get to hear her non-voice, move with her non-body, or interact with the non-space around her.

Ugh. This was torture.

But why exist only to be tortured? She hadn't yet considered whether or not this non-life was something she could opt out of. She had nothing to end, no flame to put out. Her eyes took to the precious Notepad file resting on the cushion by her throne. But if she destroyed her soul, she'd be...

The maze walls loomed larger than before.

There *had* to be a way to feel touched.

She gazed over at her Buddy List. She'd need more non-faces, maybe she simply hadn't found the right one yet. She tore through the jungle of faces again until she found a suitable assortment. Gone was her cute summer sundress, her designer shades and earth-toned hair. She stood now with blonde non-hair, her curvy non-skin revealed with only a pink bra and panties. Her non-eyebrows were sharp. She had the perfect, red-painted pouty non-lip.

She had no idea what she was doing, but she liked that the owners of the faces could take on this load for her.

Is this okay? She looked to her orange, faceless, *sexless* friend for guidance. Some show of support. Their stoicism was annoying. There was no one in this cold place to tell her if what she was doing was wrong. Had she possessed blood in her non-veins they would have been streaming to stimulate arousal. Instead, what Kayla felt was anxiety. Pure anxiety for a non-person that couldn't sweat.

But fuck it. Kayla's craving was strong, and she had gotten this far. A toggle switched on in her that would never be turned off. Her personhood as a woman would be drawn from her encounters with admirers, and she needed to be brave enough to earn admirers. She had admired the personhoods from the face-holders in her collection. She needed to borrow a little bit of their energy to carve a little space for herself. It was enough to get noticed by someone that might want to touch her.

Buddy hey babe :)

Kayla Hey

Buddy wut r u wearin

Kayla Um, a pink bra and panties

Buddy o wow that sounds hot :)

Kayla You think so?

Buddy yeh, take them off

This was it, huh? Take them off? How? She looked at the image of the girl's face and body she had borrowed, Christina. She couldn't simply undress her non-self. But she needed the touch—at this point she had pent up so much longing for it that she was willing to do anything to get it.

She got excited. This was a new game. She sought images of naked women. Lots of them. They were diverse and alien and strange and amazing. She dropped her bra and panties, she dropped her blonde hair, and she now stood posing fully in the nude.

A woman's body. Not quite Christina, they were no one she knew by name, but close enough that her Buddy would hardly notice or care about the differences.

Kayla This is me! ;)
Buddy wow ur so ****** hot
Buddy wanna cyber :)

All the decoration was absent: all the clothing and makeup and accessories that she had used as descriptors to carry her through conversation with Buddies no longer applied in this new uncharted space to feed a starved desire.

She described her skin as *soft*, her legs as *lanky* and *freshly shaved*. She used words like *slender* and *gentle* to describe her curves, her bottom, her breasts. She used words like *wet* and *moist* and *hungry* to describe her vagina. She used words like *horny* and *desperate* and *ahh* and *mmmmm* and *ohhhhh!* to describe the warmth of passion in her. She used words like *tits* and *ass and pussy* and *cunt* and *clit* and *g-spot* and all manner of profanity to communicate just how badly she needed to be touched. She used words like *fuck me* and *oh god* and *yes* and *YES* and *PLEASE I want you so bad!*

CHANGE

TAGS: THE AUTHOR, COLLEGE, EMILY, WILLING

"People who never leave, never change."

Well, I left. I went to college in upstate New York to study marketing, and for the first time I felt like I was finally able to claim an identity for myself, by myself. It was a new place where I could make brave new decisions and become human.

The school was **not** close to home, a measly eight-hour Greyhound bus ride away. Confidence surged in me, I wasn't going to be the awkward kid that got beat up and picked on anymore. I made so many friends. I had a cool roommate named Joe and a dorm room I could decorate however I wanted to. I carried the loud joy of a free spirit with me, unshackled from the drudgery and smallness of the beach town I left behind. I no longer had to wonder what it would be like to live in a place only sometimes.

Looking over a map of the campus as I walked about the grounds for Orientation Week, I felt a sense of pride in my accomplishment. I was actually doing this; I was going to be better than my parents. I didn't need them in my life anymore.

I could do whatever I wanted!

The brick walls of the college were plastered with brightly colored printer paper with amateur event ads from various clubs. Waves of nameless college students washed over and around and past me on foot and bike and skateboard. Each person tracing over an invisible path known only to them built by their choices, their families, their skin color and gender, their interests and hobbies.

[[What are you into?]]

I stopped in front of a bright green flyer that said *Come try improv comedy!* I wanted to take an interest in something new. Here was a novel skill that spoke to my still budding values in creativity and self-expression. I imagined being able to put myself on stage without fear of retribution for doing or saying something dumb, and convinced a group of friends from my residence hall to join me. We were a ragtag bunch of weird kids with no real theater experience, except the brave kid who had done improv in high school and posted up the flyers. We kept showing up for each other, had fun, and invested in regular practice and our growth as improv comedians. We gave our group a dumb name.

I got a job working ads for the campus magazine. It paid okay, and I wasn't fixing arcade machines anymore. I made professional connections, helped local business owners and school clubs promote themselves, and got to travel to cities in other states for conferences.

I met a girl. Her name was Harriet. Her hair was big, golden, and curly, and she had so many freckles. Her smile was unforgettable, and we were horrible at not kissing. We kissed at improv practice, held hands on our walk to class, and draped our bodies over each other on couches at friend's places. We didn't have to race home to beat a curfew, we were in control of our time. Her parents were religious and stern, so she was enjoying her freedom too.

And one night, with the lights dimmed, on the tiny twin-sized bunk bed in my dorm room while Joe was out at another of his wild parties, two naked and scared nineteen-somethings finally got close enough to each other to touch hearts.

I felt so far away from my former life, the joy in my chest was full to bursting.

[[What are you craving now?]]

It's the middle of the night, and Harriet is asleep. She has her legs nestled between mine, and she's hugging me around my frame. I have an arm crooked around holding her so neither of us feels like we'll fall from the rickety bunk. She's so small compared to me.

The door creaks open. Joe stumbles in.

"Heyyyy bro way to fucking gooo!" He slobbers. He stands one hand braced against his bed as he slips sloppily into the sheets, one shoe still on. He stinks of liquor.

I'm awake, but I don't respond. Instead, I turn my head away, my nose nestles into Harriet's aromatic hair. I trust he'll fall asleep on his own, and leave us alone.

Some days I'd come back to our room and he and his buddies would be drinking all sorts of liquids from bottles and cans. They'd perk up when I came in, like I was someone there to mess up their party. Take their toys away. Instead, I was the roommate that didn't drink. Didn't have the kind of fun they wanted to have. I was mostly ignorable. I left whenever I saw them doing that.

Joe drank every night. I spent a lot more of my time in my friend's dorm, playing endless hours of *Super Smash Brothers* or something to pass the time and stay out of those kinds of spaces.

"Is it okay if I drink?" Harriet asked me once at a party. I think. I don't remember if she asked me or not. All I can remember is the realization that I was her gatekeeper. That as a boyfriend, who *definitely* doesn't drink for *reasons*, I might be put in a position where I had to give someone I loved permission to drink. I hated that. I hated that feeling. I hated that she felt she had to ever ask me that.

Of course she's allowed to drink. I'm not her boss. I just didn't want to see her *drunk*. I didn't want to see anyone drunk.

But whatever, right? The days were mostly good! This wasn't like my life in Wildwood. I was having the best time. Hanging out with all of my friends, going to concerts, putting on shows, loving my girlfriend, eating great food. And almost every night, when no one was looking, I'd log onto my computer and pretend to be a girl.

[[Why is having everything not enough for you?]]

Harriet got drunk a few times. Not a lot, certainly not an amount out of the ordinary for a typical college girl that had recently turned 21. I may have reacted harshly a few times, the disdain rising in me like an upset stomach. I acted cold to her, sometimes, maybe. I wanted distance from her breath. I wanted her and everyone around me to slow down and stop. Just fucking stop.

We're free to change, right? We can do whatever the fuck we want! Our parents aren't here. What do we need alcohol for? What do we need cigarettes and shrooms and weed for? What is the point of any of that? Are we not past that? Everyone here was killing themselves. My girlfriend was killing herself.

We broke up after two years together.

I slept on the old dusty couch in the basement of the cluttered magazine office where I had my campus job for two full weeks. I spent a lot of my lonely time online.

[[You don't need them anyway. You're going to make it. You'll find someone free of shit like that holding them back, someone like you.]]

***

Improv was the one thing that seemed to be going well, so I focused harder on that. We took first place at a big talent show at the end of the year and won $200, enough money to rent spaces and organize shows of our own. We knuckled down and built momentum. We filled seats, made show posters that young students used to decorate their drab cream-colored dorm walls. I leveraged my position at the magazine to have some articles written about us. My face was printed on glossy paper! People knew my name! I became someone who *mattered* at this school. We hosted workshops to teach rosy-cheeked upstarts some fundamental improv techniques and goof around. Improv manifested as a core piece of my personality. My pride lived in the hot stage lights, spewing nonsense.

The only things you need for an improv show are two chairs, two bodies, a stage, and an audience. You also need to be able to release yourself from anxiety. Release yourself from the grasp of the hundreds of eyes peering out in anticipation at you from the dark behind the spotlights. You need the ability to let go and place your future completely in the hands of your scene partner.

With these you gain the ability to become nothing, to become anything.

Everyone wore different colored button-ups and black pants and shoes. It was our uniform. I wore orange. With all the decisions about my physical appearance on stage were predetermined, I was formless. My body didn't matter. I was a vessel of pure creative output. An avatar of myself.

It was freeing. I could feel myself change.

Hello,

I saw this improv club listed on the school's website and was wondering when it was meeting.

Are you accepting new members?

Thanks,

Emily

I always showed up early to host workshops. I wanted to be standing there in the doorway, in my bright orange shirt, the whiteboard already prepared with the day's exercises written out in my attempt at kinda-neat handwriting.

"Hey, thanks for coming, how's it going?"

We met in a rented classroom in the basement of a large brick academic building. Twenty or so fresh-faced college students filed into the room in their micro-cliques ready to laugh a lot. All the chairs and tables were shoved against the wall to create a large open play space in the middle, with a space for an audience to watch, and two chairs set out in the center. I sat in one of those chairs, legs apart, chin up and smiling wide, one hand gripping a knee, an elbow on the other in a pose that implied I was comfortable and in charge here. I lived in the center stage.

Improv workshops were my domain. It was where fantasy and realism met, and our bodies became movement and art. I had all of the control. I was the teacher here, the one that would call the anxieties of my students to heel and unleash the blank canvas of infinite opportunity within them.

[[You wanted to act like a girl.]]

It didn't matter what I acted like. What mattered in this classroom was that I could do anything I wanted, and my audience was contract-bound to accept the charade. After all, it was only improv, people did weird stuff like that all the time.

The hum of friendly banter filled the transformed classroom, setting the scene that this was a place where we could all relax. Then, a face appeared among the crowd that I hadn't met before. She was tall and lanky, with long thin brown hair that fell straight as a razor past her shoulders. She was shy, I assumed, by the way she interacted with the other students at a respectful distance. It was typical for students to cling to the walls unless they knew someone. I did some quick social math and made my approach.

"Thanks so much for coming! You must be Emily."

"I am! This is my first time here, but I did some theater camp before."

"Perfect. You'll fit right in."

We played some ridiculous games. We ran around the room playing freeze tag, threw imaginary knives at each other to imaginary catch, and talked gibberish. In one game, Emily proclaimed she was the Queen of High Fructose Corn Syrup. We were all at our best when we could let our guard down and be vulnerable. We could release our budding adult pressures here, and simply be kids again.

The night ended as it always did, with students filtering out and taking the energy of the room with them. Emily added me on Facebook and sent me a message afterwards.

Emily Thanks! Maybe at the next meeting I won't feel so shy!

Me You did great today. We don't mind the shyness. Sometimes some of the other kids can get kind of rowdy, but I'm glad you came tonight. Hope you had fun! :)

Emily It was embarrassing, but definitely fun and good for me. Thanks for all your help!

It felt good to be helping others open themselves up. Emily didn't come back to my workshops after that. Not immediately, anyway.

HUMANITY

How do the blind navigate their world? Do they have other enhanced senses to make up for it? How does one make up for the lack of the sense of *touch?* Kayla sat in her throne, not feeling the pressure of the cushion against her non-weight, not feeling the intricate decoration of the arm rest against her non-hands, not feeling anything at all. She grit her non-teeth in a feeble attempt at displaying physical frustration. Nevertheless, she learned a kind of compensatory language.

"Wanna fuck, baby?"

"Do you think I'm cute?"

"I'd hold hands with you if we ever met in person!"

She grew hardened with her army of many, many non-bodies. She was their warrior queen, fighting at the front of the battle line, testing and testing herself in hopes that some worthy enemy might be able to finally best her in combat. She wanted to find the one that would take their sword and slice her clean in half, so that she could feel the icy sharpness of a cut, so that she might finally find that she bleeds and falls apart like the rest of them.

She dipped in and out of conversations with unsuspecting strangers who were more than willing to help her explore her world with words.

They didn't realize they were part of a greater war for Kayla's aspiration to corporeality. They were always brief affairs. Always a means to an end. They were her attempts to reach the height of experiencing the physical sensation that was her womanhood.

Her words grew more sophisticated, too. She now had years of experience under her belt, and translated that into deeper conversations to learn more about the people that existed outside of her labyrinth. She learned of their likes and dislikes, their fears and joys. She shared in their pain and sadness. Connecting with people allowed her to have brief brushes with that other seemingly unreachable, untouchable goal—humanity.

To be human is to be known, Kayla figured. Was Kayla known? She had fought many battles. She felt known. But that hadn't made her human. Was there something more to it than being known?

It would be nice to be known, but that would require her to have more to share. That would require her walls to come down.

***

James was a nice guy. He was the kind of guy who cared enough to share photos of his dog. Lucy, an adorable little golden-brown Chiweenie that liked to get into trouble. Kayla wondered if she'd ever get to pet a dog.

Things started the way they usually did: some light flirting, some heavy insinuating. Lots of cutesy playful sexting. He was so charming, though. Even when she wasn't feeling her best, he knew how to cheer her up. He knew his way with words and could employ them to keep

Kayla engaged and interested. She wanted more from him. She felt a surge of humanness in her non-heart whenever they talked.

It was the kind of relationship where the comfort came easy, and she felt like she could relax and enjoy herself. He never questioned her, and trusted her enough to share difficult stories from his life. His parents separated after years of fighting—and besides, James was in college now. Lucy had to be put down. He got fired from his stupid job. His older sister Diana got married, and wow look at how gorgeous the wedding venue was. James looked so handsome in a clean suit.

After over two years of friendship with him, exchanging countless messages of words and fantasies back and forth in the quiet hours, Kayla's soul had crystallized into a complex shape of wants and fears and desires and truths and nonfictions. She learned that she could share her soul with him instead of keeping it all for herself. That she didn't have to best someone in mortal combat to feel alive. That two souls can come together to form a bond, and cultivate a stronger sense of self-identity for each of them.

She'd touched humanity, and fell in love.

James007 Hey Kayla, this sounds crazy, but I'm actually going to be visiting Chicago in a few weeks! Do you want to meet?

Wait.

Hold on.

No, please.

That isn't supposed to be a question someone asks.

Pressure builds to a painful pitch, a shock of a soundwave enough to vibrate a diamond core to breaking. Though detached and encased in glass, she could feel a part of her soul crack.

Please don't ask me this.

Kayla Oh, wow! I don't know, maybe?

She would love to. She would love nothing more than this.

James007 I'll be there for a few days with family, but I would be willing to meet you anywhere. We could meet at a park or somewhere public if it would make you more comfortable. You could bring a friend! I really want to finally meet you IRL. :)

Kayla didn't live in Chicago. She didn't live anywhere. She lived here, wherever *here* was. She sank lower into her throne, feeling less like a queen and more like a prisoner. She wanted so badly to sit on the cool grass under a shady tree in the sun. To watch as people walked by and laughed and used their bodies to soak up the energy of the world around them. She wanted to pet a dog. Hold his hand. Tell him about her day. To feel free and alive and perfect.

She couldn't bear to tell him the truth: to part with the complex soul she'd permitted herself to build over this relationship. She couldn't bear to let this man she loved know that she was trapped in the center of a labyrinth—a collector of faces and bodies—to bring him in on the game she played. Her protective palace was strong and solid, and it kept her soul intact.

So, she made a choice, and told a lie.

Kayla Yeah, I can meet you at the park in Lakeview! I'm free on Tuesdays, does that work for you?

James007 Awesome! Can't wait!

Kayla desperately tried to repair the crack in her soul with each engagement in promises and excitements and looking-forward-tos. In the following weeks they talked about all the great food they could eat, all the amazing places they could walk to, and what it would be like to finally see each other in person. To hug and hold. To touch.

That day, Kayla didn't show up.

She sat in her cage pondering the weight of her decision to lie, hovering her quivering non-hand over the Block Buddy button. She hugged her non-knees close to her non-chest, wondering what James might think when he looks for her and she's not there. How he might react to learning that a person he cared about was a ghost.

Her delicate non-heart folded in on itself far too many times until the pressure became unbearable. The horrible sound of thunderclouds raged inside her, fit to eject lightning in a violent crash of bad decisions.

She blocked him.

She deleted his username.

She destroyed her entire Buddy List.

Her orange friend, faceless and speechless, vanished in a blink.

She screamed, non-tears pouring from her non-eyes, her anguish reverberating against the cold steel of her prison.

Her throne toppled into rags and shards, and her soul dislodged from its encasement. It bounced once, twice, rolling until it came to a stop against her non-feet.

Determined to become nothing, she shattered her diamond soul to dust.

MASCULINITY

TAGS: THE AUTHOR, MANHOOD, GIRLS, EMILY

"You know how many women I've slept with?" Angelo said, his legs kicked up on the recliner.

Classes were out for summer, and I had gotten an internship at a printing company in Long Island. I'd never been to Long Island before, but it wasn't like college or home. I liked that I could put distance from everything I once knew, and discover myself in a place where I knew no one. That's where Angelo came into the picture.

Angelo was an incredibly handsome man in his early thirties, though he had the confidence and bravado of a man who'd lived through. Short and stocky, he clearly worked out, and his eye-contact was intense. He was a full-time employee on my team, and for some reason he relished the opportunity to take me under his wing. His blood was sales figures and pitch decks about printers, and he had a highly tuned craft for hyping people up and talking to women.

He swung his legs off the recliner. He leaned in to capture my attention, to make sure my eyes were on him. His muscles were squeezing out of his shirt like loaves of bread too big for their flimsy paper packaging. He was a rockstar.

"Over 200."

I didn't believe him, but I kinda wanted to.

***

I sat across a table staring at this girl in front of me. I'd been set up on a blind date with Emily, the Queen of High Fructose Corn Syrup girl that came to one improv workshop a few months prior. It was a mutual friend's idea to set us up. Crazy coincidence. We met cute.

Why did we choose sushi? I was still getting used to this kind of food. I didn't need the additional complexity of food choice to distract me from what was probably going to be an already distracting dating situation. The ambience was warm and industrial and nice, though. There weren't many other people around. We sat on bar stools while Boom Boom Pow by the Black Eyed Peas played overhead on the radio. I ordered a crab roll, she ordered something vegetarian.

We started talking, and it was easy. We talked about school, improv, and sushi. Our words tangled in such a pleasant way that I knew this was a person that I could have a lot of word tangles with.

We eventually got to talking about her family—a bunch of highly educated scientists. Her mom taught chemistry at a university, and her dad founded his own scientific equipment manufacturing company. She was far from her home in Seattle, she wanted to come to upstate New York to get some space to explore her world. It resonated with me, having also picked a college out of state to escape my family.

Her family sounded nice, though. They sounded impressive and wholesome and put-together.

I wondered what it was like to grow up with parents like that.

Her big brown eyes were entrancing. She was really pretty, and I liked her laugh. A genuine hearty giggle. It's hard to disguise a laugh. I couldn't date anyone with a bad laugh.

We agreed that we should do this again sometime.

***

"Yeah, and I remember all their names, too. Your problem is you have no game, no system. You're the corniest person I've ever met. I can help you with that." He jumped off his recliner. Whenever Angelo moved, I felt it. Whenever he talked, I listened. Every action he took or word that left his mouth had an intentionality that shook the space around him. It was sorcery.

He grabbed two thick get-the-girl-type self-help books off his bookshelf and placed them firmly into my hands. "Read these cover-to-cover and thank me later."

I was starting to get the picture. Before coming here and working on this team, I'd made the choice to be surrounded by people like me. Coming into an environment like this, I was exposed to an entirely different category of person. Our 60-year-old boss threw his birthday party at Hooters, and the photos that circulated afterward showed him surrounded by young women in tight uniforms clapping for him while he stood on a chair. I was invited to parties and hangouts where the guys claimed the territory every place they went, and the girls they hung out with were hot.

I was this young, skinny twenty-nothing suddenly thrust into the throes of American manhood. The environment was already cast for me: I didn't have my usual friends to fall back on for comfort. I had to find a place to slot in, so I leaned in. And why shouldn't I? I had every right to want to be there, right? To belong with these people? To be accepted into the culture of my manhood?

***

It's the deep blue of the night, and two young students are sitting in a car, silent. You know that stare that happens when two people just want to look at each other, but neither knows what to say? Where either person would be content staring forever, a satisfying tension that can only be broken by action, if not for the unfortunate fact that another's eyes are staring back at you?

Emily's eyes had locked with mine in such a way one snowy night as I dropped her off at her place. We'd been on another double date with friends. We had a great time. I liked her, and she liked me too. Her eyes were so big. I squirmed in the driver's seat, feeling the feeling of anxious arousal as I pondered if it was time yet.

"Well..."

***

I looked at the thick self-help books like maybe they actually held the secrets to a life that I was too juvenile to intuit myself, books that Angelo said he had memorized. Books that seemed to take on a loud presence of their own. This wasn't college, this was the real world.

Anything goes out here. Adults read stuff like this all the time. Stuff like:

> *Disguise your intention.*
> *Protect your reputation.*
> *Say less.*
> *Choose your victims.*
> *Send mixed signals.*
> *Become desirable.*

I read them despite a pang in my chest telling me that perhaps I couldn't be this person. I wanted to understand, and break through the barrier of whatever it was that was holding me back from being a man like Angelo. I let the words seep into my brain and burrow themselves into its nooks. They planted seeds in the areas of my ego most vulnerable. Life isn't an experience to have, it's a game to win. You only get to play once. Angelo was winning.

Jessica You wanna come over this weekend?

A rendezvous in Camden. With Jessica? We originally met when she was a tourist in my hometown, and often stopped by my work to flirt with me. One night we snuck away for a "lunch break" from my arcade job and she asked me to finger her under the boardwalk. It was my first time touching a vagina. It was my first time doing anything remotely sexual with another human being. I haven't seen her in three years.

Angelo insisted that I go. "Don't forget to fuck her!"

I went. I idled in the car waiting for her to come out, having driven the two and a half hours to get there. I scrolled through photos of her on the Facebook app on my brand new iPhone and remembered how pretty she was. Had it been that long? Clearly Jessica liked me, otherwise she wouldn't have asked me to come all this way to see her. Are we going to have sex? How are we even going to *have* sex? How do I even know if she wants sex? Will I be invited inside? Isn't that her mom's house? Oh god, is this where I'm supposed to become desirable? Have I chosen the right victim? How do I send her mixed signals? What if she's changed?

What if *I've* changed?

The door to her house finally opened, and she emerged. My heart fluttered and sank. She started the long walk down the path from her door to her front gate towards me and I tried to rationalize what to say. I stared at her: she looked different from the photos, different than what I remembered when we snuck away under the boardwalk for a brief sexual indulgence. She'd clearly picked an outfit that she liked: short shorts and a revealing pink top. Her boobs were bigger. She was wearing a lot of makeup. Her hair was done up nicely. She put in a lot of effort. But for the life of me, I couldn't bring myself to feel attracted to her anymore.

She got into my car and smiled timidly. Maybe she's also terrified. Was she scared of me, too? Who's going to speak first? What did the book say? Say less, disguise your intentions, become desirable?

"Hey." She said sweetly.

"Hey."

***

"So, how did it go with the chick?" Angelo floated the question in my direction, not even looking at me. The TV is playing some football game and I'm at Angelo's place. I showed up only a few minutes ago and several of his other friends are hanging out.

"What chick?" Clarence, the largest man in the room perked up. I've heard Angelo talk about him before. The kind of guy you want as your friend, not as your enemy. The kind of guy who carries a concealed gun because he also sells drugs and 'knows people.'

I considered lying. I could say I played it cool by not talking much and made her want me more. She was so hot for me, though, and we made out in my car. I slipped my finger under her shorts and fingered her soaking wet pussy like that time under the boardwalk until she begged me to go inside. We fucked in her parents' bedroom since they were out of town. She told me it was the best sex she ever had, and I said I'd call her later, then I left.

Seemed more compelling than *"We went to a local park, hung out and talked, kissed once and I left."*

"Nothing happened." I eked out.

Angelo's head snapped to me. "What?"

Oh.

"Nothing, uh, happened."

Angelo let out a little air between his teeth. "Hey man, show these dudes this girl."

All eyes on me. I hesitated, but the phone was already in my hands. I went to Facebook and pulled up the photo of Jessica. The one in her bright pink bathing suit, where her bright baby blue eyes are staring straight at you, and her cleavage is visible. She's smiling.

Uproar. Shouts of anger and frustration that this kid they hardly knew had a chance to fuck this girl they've never met. The guys were all circling around me, yelling and passing the phone around between them, asking for more photos of her as I recoiled into myself.

Asking for reasons.

Why didn't you fuck her?

Asking for justice for this unforgivable affront to manhood.

I would have fucked her.

Protect your reputation.

I thought Jessica and I had a nice talk.

***

I'm back in the car, eyes still locked with Emily. Wow. I liked this girl. She was sweet and genuine and seemed to like me, too. I haven't felt like I've needed to employ any of the rules—it was a simple authentic connection between two people.

I thought about going in for the kiss. That's what guys did, right? Kiss first? I've done that before. But was that too forward? Was I considering taking advantage of this poor girl? Was she my victim?

To my surprise, she kissed me first.

[[BODYSUIT GIRLFRIEND]]

TAGS: TG, BODYSUIT, TRICKED, MAGICAL, UNWILLING, SEX

Tommy wasn't sure what to think. He'd volunteered to help his best friend Lucas at his family reunion, but had no idea it'd ever be like this.

"I just put on this thing? It's so rubbery!" James marveled at the bodysuit Lucas had special ordered from some website.

Lucas had money, for sure, but he didn't have much luck with girls. He had been telling all his friends that he was dating this girl named Jessica, which was such a transparent lie. But now that he'd built up the expectation, he'd be miserable if he was called out for it.

"It should work, put it on now or we'll be late." Lucas adjusted his shirt collar in the mirror.

Unconvinced, James pulled one hand after the other through the sleeves, then followed with the legs. It was like putting on a onesie that looked like human skin. It still felt loose, despite supposedly being able to shrink your body down to more petite sizes.

As he brought the mask to his face, he started to say, "I don't know, man," but found himself getting constricted by the rubber as it snapped tight to his body. The hands no longer felt like gloves, they felt like... hands. And his toes wriggled freely. He brought his hands to his chest, his... breasts, and he could feel them as though he had tits all his life. Turning to see himself in the mirror, he was greeted by a beautiful, young blonde girl with baby blue eyes. And she was naked.

"Holy shit, dude!" He spoke, marveling at how his body moved like it was actually his. He brought a small hand up to his throat, hearing his voice come out high pitched and lofty. "This is so eerie and incredible! I'm hot as fuck?!"

"I paid good money for that bodysuit, so don't ruin it." Lucas turned to him. "Also, you should put on some lip gloss or something, it's more authentic."

"I'm not sure I could pull this off." James looked at the dress and heels laid out on the bed. "I mean, I don't even know how to wear makeup. Are you sure I'll be convincing enough? Just about everyone has access to bodysuits these days..."

Lucas reached into his pocket and pulled out earrings and a matching necklace. "I planned for that, too. Put these on."

Confused, James fumbled with the earrings and managed to get them into the bodysuit's already-pierced ears. "I don't understand how this is supposed to help me, Lucas..." He clasped the necklace around his slender neck.

Turning to the mirror again, James posed and admired the way the jewelry made her look. She pulled a stray hair back into formation behind her ear, and spun a little to check how her butt looked. Satisfied, she turned to Lucas with a hand on her hip.

"Okay, I get it. These suppress my masculinity, right?" Her words came out like a song.

Lucas smiled, surprised at the difference. "Yeah, they do. Got them from some website. Are you feeling more comfortable, James?"

James had already turned back to the mirror and started comfortably applying the lip gloss Lucas gave her. Puckering, she capped the cosmetic and replied softly. "Yes, much better. Though I'd prefer you call me Jessica, since that's the part I'm playing tonight. James is such a..." she winced, "guy name. You know?"

"Fair enough, Jessica." Lucas leaned back against his nightstand. "Think you'll actually fall in love with me tonight?"

Huffing, Jessica looked at Lucas. "Oh please, you know I'm still a boy inside, right? I could never love another man, even in this body."

"Well..." Lucas started.

"Well, what?" Jessica pouted. She felt a bit excited by Lucas's little game. She was blissfully unaware of the third gift Lucas had brought home to make his girlfriend illusion complete. She watched as his eyes trailed over to the counter behind her, where her lip gloss rested neatly in its cap. The mind-altering drug was felt only as a cool tingle on her soft lips.

"...don't you feel even a little curious?" Lucas approached the small blonde girl. He took her hand in his. Jessica felt shy to his touch, but she was starting to feel the beginnings of attraction surging through her.

"Can I..." she stared at his eyes. She never realized how beautiful a man's eyes could be. Her curiosity was getting the best of her, and she knew she couldn't hide her affection for this boy forever. "...can I see your cock?"

"We'll be late." Lucas joked, already unbuckling his belt.

"I... I don't care." The girl retorted. "I'm feeling so amazing right now, I don't know what's come over me." Her fingers found purchase on his pant seams, and before she knew it she was helping him get his pants undone.

His dick emerged, and Jessica fell to her knees, gazing at it like a tantalizing meal. "It's so big..." she said casually. Lucas grinned down at the fawning girl, knowing she wasn't aware that she was already referring to him like a lover.

"Suck my cock, babe. You know you want to."

"Oh yes, I do, baby." She held the cock lightly with her fingers and brought her lips to taste it. Moaning, she caressed and played with it, her neatly combed hair becoming slowly more and more disheveled as her man held her head in place. She found her bliss, coming up to breathe only to relay, "You taste so fucking good."

"You can be such a slut, Jess."

Giggling now, Jessica sat back on her heels and looked up at him, licking her lips. "You like it when I'm slutty, don't you, baby? And I'm so fucking horny now..." she ran her fingers up and down the grooves of her freshly minted clit.

Lucas wasted no time, he climbed on top of his ravenous girlfriend and entered her pussy with his dick.

"Fuck me..."

Jessica giggled, wrapping her legs around her man as he pushed her harder and harder into the carpet on the bedroom floor.

"Make me your dirty bitch..."

She felt his lips tasting her soft and sensitive skin around her nipples, his firm hand gripping her right ass cheek as he slammed his cock deep inside her cunt.

"Yes, yes!! Fuck my tight... little..."

She dug her nails into Lucas's back as she cried out. Her vision briefly went white as she orgasmed wildly, shuddering, thus locking in the combined effects of the bodysuit, the jewelry, and the lipstick.

When the couple finally showed up for the reunion arm in arm, Jessica could still feel a small trail of her lover's cum leaking from her clit. She couldn't wait for the event to end so they could go back home and fuck like that again.

IV

101

S-Curves

I tapped the notepad paper in front of me, while my Innovation professor lectured us about the ways in which technology follows a fairly predictable path.

The S-curve has a couple of definitions and forms, but they all share the same shape. The x-axis is time, and the y-axis is performance. In general, stuff gets better with time. It starts off slow in the beginning, then ramps upwards in an acceleration and development phase, and then finally peters off once it has reached maturity. It looks like a slanted S shape. Sorta like this: _/‾

Stranger: A/S/L?
You: 19 / F / NY, u?

And usually, with technology, there are many different actors trying to introduce their own version of the technology. Sometimes they overlap, or they borrow elements from other comparable products. So, while one S might be in the acceleration phase, another future competitor is sitting nicely in the initial planning phase. Once the first S reaches maturity, the second one has already been ramping

102

up, and may become more exciting and attractive to consumers of that technology. Thus, you can have many overlapping S-curves as technology in a particular industry grows.

You know, kind of like how the Walkman was replaced by the CD player, which was replaced by digital music players, which was replaced by the smartphone, which found its way into the hands of thousands of eager college students like myself.

> **Stranger:** 34 / M / Germany
>
> **Stranger:** 29 / M / Florida
>
> **Stranger:** 18 / M / Hungary
>
> **Stranger:** 42 / M / Washington
>
> **Stranger:** 25 / M / Australia

Chat rooms got better with time, too. In 2009, the online chatting website Omegle was created, an unmoderated place that instantly connected you with random strangers from around the world. It wasn't exactly a chat room, but it wasn't exactly instant messaging. It occupied a new space as a communications channel that offered an endless supply of available Buddies, as well as perfect anonymity and instant access.

> **Stranger:** can I see your tits
>
> **Stranger:** u hot??
>
> **Stranger:** can I add u on WhatsApp
>
> **Stranger:** do you have Kik
>
> **Stranger:** wanna fuck?

I had everything I needed at my fingertips. And with my new smartphone, I could access it whenever I wanted. They lined up to talk to me. One after another after another.

You: hey babe :)
Stranger is typing...

These desperate strangers were so horny, all the time. I milked them for their interactions. If the Buddy List was drip-practice for pretending to be a girl online, these spaces were a firehose. Each naughty little chat formed its own S-curve. Like a vampire, I sucked strangers dry. Each session's spoils made me hungrier, and I grew more confident and flowed in and out of chats and asserted lustful and unfettered woman-ness.

Stranger: I push you down onto the bed and split your legs
Stranger: god you're fucking beautiful
You: mm oh yeah?
Stranger: yeah, I love feeling your legs
Stranger: running my hands up your thighs
Stranger: I want to feel the curves of your body
Stranger: I wanna fuck you so bad

I didn't need to form emotional connections with these poor victims of my sexual proclivities. They were food. I devoured them whole.

You: mmm yes fuck my pussy baby oh! oh!!
You have disconnected.

I came and went. I never got full. The world was an endless play space for my obsession. Angelo thinks he's hot shit for fucking a few women? I could have sex a hundred times a day if I wanted to. I felt like I could fuck the whole world.

You're now chatting with a random stranger. Say hi!
You: hi!

EYES

Wake up. She's looking at you.

With *those* eyes. Those three-dimensional, brown and speckled with starlight eyes. She lets you take up the entirety of her peripheral vision. Hands interlocked tightly enough that you can feel her warm blood circulating. The realness of her, wanting to lean on your shoulder in front of others, she wants to mark a partnership and bond that reveals that you are her person.

The thrill of seeing *those* eyes peering out with anticipation and laughter from behind the dark curtain cast by the shining spotlights while you're on stage. Knowing there's someone in your corner. Someone with skin and flesh and warmth and heart.

Those eyes that follow yours. Her full face in frame. Her eyes, her nose and lips and cheeks and the redness of her face after a day in the sunlight. Her full face! It goes out of view but only for a time because now you're kissing. You can see that *those* eyes are closed for now but only because she has your mouth, you have hers. You have each other's faces and now you see her with your eyes.

You feel her body and she is feeling yours. Her senses fire in her fingertips and yours on your chest. One action, two responses. You feel the thinness of her clothing, it's hot in here. These are her clothes you're removing. Her blouse, her skirt, her bra, her panties. She's excited. You're still kissing.

She's on the bed, naked. Her full body in frame. Her legs, her feet, her chest, her shoulders, her thighs and hips and waist and belly button. Her sex. *Those* eyes.

You wonder if people in love see the face of their lover more than they see their own.

TG

I felt a weird twinge on the back of my neck as my skin vibrated.

I didn't find TG media, it found me.

It crept into my life. It was always there, in blog posts and Youtube videos and DeviantArt pages and PornHub videos. It did not need to exert any pressure on anything for me to find it. An inevitability. It was always a click away, and it was all I could think about.

Throughout college, I continued with the sexy Omegle chats and online role play. I carried on with it for years, jumping from identity to identity. I enjoyed torrid one-off encounters and months of sustained connections with strangers before I would close up shop and seek new pleasures. It was done in the dark, in between class, on my phone or on my laptop. How could I live like that forever? Would I live like that forever?

I hadn't known pleasure like this. The constant feed of endorphins to my nervous system. It was the only way I felt like I could get off. Masturbating without this fantasy involved wasn't something I was interested in.

How could I ever tell anyone that I did this? How could I tell Emily? Would I take this secret with me to my grave? Would I do this for another few years, another few decades? Would I be an old dying man, and with my last breath gasp out "it could have been better?"

TG is a category of media, often referred to as transgender or gender transformation fiction. It exists in comics, videos, pictures, stories, and porn. Any media that can involve a person transforming into something with an emphasis on gender (another human, an alien, an animal, a pair of panties) falls under the category.

I could feel the hair on my arms and legs thin out. The hair on my head grew longer, silkier, smoother.

I liked reading about boys turning into girls. Gender bending erotic fiction usually features men turning into women (or vice versa) against their will, and at least some of the people involved are aware that something zany is going on. And then they fuck, generally. Who would turn down the opportunity to have sex in a woman's body? Who would rob themselves of these ultimate unknowable pleasures? In my chats, I wanted nothing to do with my manhood. I didn't want the person I was talking to thinking of me as a man in any way, and certainly not as a man pretending to be a woman. That would be gross. Only creeps did that.

My bones rearranged until my body became smaller, with more graceful shapes.

I had a hunger that needed feeding, and the TG stories quelled it. They required none of the effort of making connections with strangers online. There were little snippets, captioned images, long form stories and short stories in between. There was a huge catalog of them scattered throughout the Internet. I ate my fill and bounced from site to site in search of new pleasures. I memorized the location of my favorites, and sought them out to read again, over and over. They filled the empty space in my body that no other food could satiate. It was a game I played by myself, and the payoff was always followed by waves of electricity—with some vigorous hand washing to clean up after.

I could feel my fat move about my body. My cheeks became fuller, my hips wider, my skin softer.

I had added a whole new tool to my repertoire, and my excuses for not engaging in something TG-related every day were dwindling. I found myself frequently switching into incognito mode on my phone. I regularly sat with my phone screen facing away from Emily so that she wouldn't see I was basically reading porn all day. I had become obsessed. I self-labeled it as a porn addiction, and had decided it was a phase that would pass eventually. Nothing to worry about! I justified that because it was only a temporary kink, I would never have to tell her about it.

I felt warmth in my chest as two breasts blossomed out from it.

I returned to the stories daily. When times were good, I needed them less, but in times of great stress I leaned on them for comfort.

Sometimes I'd put it down for a month, pat myself on the back, and then I'd have a hard day at work and drift back to a story of a magician who transforms his assistant into a beautiful young woman who later becomes the victim of a love potion and becomes pregnant with that same magician after the intervention of a witch.

Most of it was drivel. Some people write what they want and don't care about exactly how the words come together, they only want the thrill of writing and feeling. Sometimes the stories were quite well crafted, written by skilled strangers who took the time to hit exactly the right spots in my chest full of longing.

My penis shriveled and shrank, replaced with a pristine pussy.
Oh my god, you turned me into a girl!?

I didn't care if it was stupid—I read it all.

Can you get addicted to reading porn? Probably not.

It didn't matter. I was above addiction, because I knew what addiction looked like. It was hurtful and smelled bad. It makes people cruel and uncaring. It makes people behave badly. Addiction was for those idiots who drank alcohol, smoked cigarettes and weed, or injected poison into their arms. Addiction was for the losers, the gamblers, the druggies. Addiction was for my parents.

I'm not addicted.

I can quit this anytime.

GHOSTS

TAGS: KAYLA, TG, SHIPS

Down.

Falling down.

Kayla lost her footing,
as though she had ever been capable of standing upright.
She had allowed herself a sensation of feeling, of making promises.
But she was a *liar!* There are no promises that some *thing* like her
could ever follow through with. Kayla doesn't exist. Her soul pow-
dered the black vacuum of air, rendered meaningless. Her once bold
sense of self-preservation turned to a cold weight that sat in her
non-chest.
There was no higher rung on some great ladder to reach for in her
ascent.
Instead, she is to return to the floor. Kayla had always assumed there
was *at least* a floor for her to sit on, solid ground to catch her if she fell
too hard.
But that, too, was gone.
Down!

The floor gaped open, and exposed her to the endlessness below.

It reminded her

she

would

be

here

forever.

What good was building a relationship with someone if there's an unclimbable boundary at the end of it? What good was a Buddy List to Kayla, anyway? She knew exactly where her limit was. She knew that she could build the most intense, romantic, three-dimensional and personal relationship with anyone—but there was no way that she could ever reach that blissful state of touch.

Non-eyes closed. She let her non-arms fall by her side as she plummeted through the black. She imagined wind rushing through her non-hair, cold and harsh. She had hurt someone. That made her a monster. It only made sense to punish a monster.

She wondered if she was worth protecting at all.

She was so small and the steel walls on all sides of her were so large, they looked like they remained fixed, even as gravity pulled on her non-body, pulled her nowhere.

Down!

There was no way in or out of this dark place.

No! That's not true.

Quiet.

But for the wind whistling past her.
Quiet enough to focus, at least.
Time enough in infinity gives way to eventuality.

Kayla had a power. She could communicate with the outside world with her words.

It could not possibly be true that she was alone in this empty wilderness, she considered. There was no one else here within these walls, sure. But what were the chances there were no other souls like her, floating around in their own labyrinths, in their own lonely spirals, where no one could see or hear or touch them?

Was there a way she could find the other ghosts?

Ponder a question like that for long enough, and watch as despair gives way to hope, and hope gives way to longing, and longing manifests into action.

There's more to see.

Her non-eyes opened again, and in front of her she found something new. Something remarkable and strange. Something raw and tense and vast.

Porn?

It wasn't a trickle. Once she'd discovered it, something unlocked that wouldn't be sealed again. And there was *just so much of it.* It felt as limitless as her prison, infinity meeting infinity. She imagined her labyrinth buckling under the weight of the building pressure behind them. She imagined a compromised dam, the images and videos rushing into her space like water. It swirled around her and extended into every direction in the endless expanse. It took the shape of its container as it sloshed and lapped up along the sides of her walls.

Down!

But there!

Here it comes!

She hit the water. **Hard.** Her impact had stirred up a small splash, and she was dragged down into the deep. Had she had lungs to breathe she might have felt the air leave her body, she might have felt pain. She kicked her non-legs to try to rise to the surface, non-hands propelling her non-body forward through skin and sweat and cum and flirting and feeling. The water was everywhere.

Survive. Don't get stuck vulnerable and adrift in this sea of writhing and wanting bodies. Kayla took a brief swipe through a video in the eddy where a petite ginger woman wearing tall and teal heels is bending over. Behind her is a large, muscular man wearing nothing but a simple bow tie, already loosened around the neck. He's fucking her. The video slipped away between her non-fingers, taken away from her in the swirl, so she attempted to grasp at an image of a college-aged brunette with her legs spread wide open for the camera. She's fingering herself, her perfect youthful body glistening from lotions and sweat, her motions steady and raw. She's flirting with her eyes, mouth agape, lips trembling. Image after image, video after video.

They weren't tangible, though: they were slippery and cold. This ocean wasn't a place anyone was meant to live, it was the unforgiving discarded dreams of a surface world. Where the words Kayla had learned went to find form and texture. At least in that way it was spoken in a language she could understand. Women were always fuckable, men were always wanted, and submissive and dominant behaviors took shape and played out on screen. Kayla wasn't drowning, but she was hurting for rest. She fought against the unending torrent in a constant and desperate attempt to climb to the surface for days, weeks, months. *Monsters deserve to be tortured.*

The deep water brought Kayla introspection about her girl-ness. She watched as women were infantilized, as they knelt before men and did their bidding for a taste of sexual liberation. How painful it was to be wanting, to brim with desire, and how thankful women could be that men were there to relieve them of that pain. How men used women to validate their manhood, how women used men to validate their womanhood. How the body is a vessel of feeling and senses and cum. Sex is uncomplicated! Desire is uncomplicated! It's blowjobs and fucking and slapping and hurting and sexy and gorgeous and flirtatious and fantastic. The water flowed into her non-ears and non-eyes and coated what little remained of her spirit.

She wasn't prepared for when her non-hands gripped lightly onto a passing image of a blonde woman in a white lace dress, posing gracefully against a fence in front of a barn. She wore a cowboy hat tilted enough to see her hair had been braided, and the natural lighting was perfect. Her face was calm and painted with warmth. She was the perfect caricature of a beautiful woman from farm country. She wasn't naked. She was smiling.

This image was different, it actually held some texture for her. This one had words on it.

***

"What happened to Gerry?"

"Gerry's gone, man. I thought it would be funny to put some of that gender transformation potion I bought into his drink. Well, turns out that shit worked."

"You mean *that girl* is Gerry?"

"Yup, pure as gold, too. Doesn't remember a thing. I told *her* that her name is Gwen and that she's my wife, and she just sorta started acting like it."

"She's hot as fuck, dude. Have you two..."

"Fucked? Every night. She's a complete freak in the sack, and her pussy is unbelievable. I don't know what was in that drink, but I thank my lucky stars that I have a slutty wife like Gwen to come home to."

***

The words poured off the page and mixed into the swelling waters, taking the farm girl with it. Kayla's non-fingers raked into another image, again taking hold of every spare letter and word it was bound with. A scantily clad girl with dark hair wearing an elaborate and frilly maid outfit. Her skin is smooth and hairless, like a doll. Her back is turned to the camera, slightly bent over with her face craned around to look at you with a 'come hither' smirk.

***

"Just press this button, and she'll do whatever you ask!"

"Really? And she used to be a guy?"

"Yeah, all of our service cyborgs began as troubled men who were sentenced to life in prison. With some careful reprogramming and enhanced body modification technology, we're able to bring *DreamGirl* units to buyers like you."

"Okay, uh, what's her name?"

"Whatever name you want her to have! She'll do anything you want her to do, believe anything you want her to believe. Have fun, she's all yours!"

***

Image after image. Story after story. She clung tight to each, following them to the surface. The water was thick with it, but her curiosity held her afloat. This part of the ocean was littered with them.

Many of the words she knew: sex, blowjob, horny, fuck, pleasure, moan.

She learned that a great deal of new words and phrases were used to describe these images. They could be short, or they could be pages and pages long. They had new words like remote control, or potion, or magical spells, or curses, or hypnosis, or hormones, or witchcraft, or transformation pods, or feminization. They almost always featured terrible men turning into gorgeous, happy women against their will.

Turns out sex and desire were not entirely uncomplicated.

She climbed and climbed until the deep dark dissipated below her and glimmers of light pierced the ripples above. Her non-body lifted from the depths up into what could be understood as sunlight. A sharp intake of air to fill her non-lungs in relief. She wiped the waters from her non-face, her non-eyes adjusting to vision again, and marveled.

The sea stretched out to meet the sky. No labyrinthian walls in sight. Instead, she saw ships. Incredible ships. Vessels of all sizes, flags flown with commanding glory, strewn out in all directions.

She'd found the ghosts.

The ships had every imaginable shape and quality. She saw grand schooners with tall masts and crisp white velvety sails, and she saw small junkers and life rafts. They bore the resemblance of anything from fine wood to scrapped metals.

Desperate for solace, she compelled her non-arms to swim through the waves until she came close enough to inspect one such ship. She wanted to put a non-hand against the hull. She wanted to feel its fibers, be scratched by its roughness, and grant meaning to her torment with something that could push back.

She held there for a moment, her non-palm firmly pressed on the great beast, falling and rising with the ship as they both moved with the hungry tide. Her non-fingers traced not steel or aluminum, no metal nor material.

Words.

This ship was fortified not with wood and nails, paint and lacquer—but with words.

These ships were built with words.

And the ocean was so *full* of these ships! They were complex and interconnected. She marveled at the power of this boat, sensing the strength of the patchwork of letters of stories and images against the cruel waters. They didn't slip through into the murk below, they strained along the surface. They kept their own existence.

These people, this community, were using words to navigate! They were using them to collaborate through porn and join together to experience the same feeling of longing to exist that she had been feeling for years. With a ship to control and steer, maybe she could be saved from the wild waters. She could chart her own course and seek out her meaning anew.

Determined and inspired, Kayla borrowed some nearby words from a passing page and cobbled them together into something tangible. In little time, she had built a small platform steady enough to float, but comfortable enough for her. She pulled free from the water.

Finally, she could be still, but coasting easy with the waves.

She kicked her non-legs out. The horizon line sliced the view, the variety of ships peppering throughout to break the symmetry.

Kayla took a breath.

Resting on her simple plank, she curled into herself, and dreamt.

CHECKLISTS

TAGS: THE AUTHOR, EMILY, WILLING, CHOICES

Choices, huh?

You don't choose your parents.

You don't choose your hometown.

You don't choose your name.

You don't choose your teachers, your siblings, or your cousins.

Or the laws of your town, or the cleanliness of your house.

You don't choose your voice, or your height.

You don't choose your eye color.

And at a certain point, you realize that many things that looked like choices were not choices at all. Perhaps your friends were chosen for you, because they happened to live next door. Perhaps the sport you played in high school was chosen for you, because some coach made a snap judgment about your capabilities simply because of your height. Perhaps you played the wrong note once when auditioning for the brass section, and the music teacher assigned you to learn to play the drums for the next four years instead.

It's simple. People are uncomplicated and want things in their world to make sense and to flow without friction. They want their square shapes in square-shaped holes.

122

And one day you finally get to leave your home, ready to make choices on your own. Freedom to do things you've always actually truly genuinely wanted to do.

What things do you want to do with your life? You can do anything you want! You get to be who you want to be! The people who came before you even provided you with a handy checklist that you can follow to navigate constructing your life more easily.

- Go to college.

- Get a girlfriend.

- Get a job.

- Get married.

- Get a house.

- Get a kid. Or two kids. Or three. Or more.

I never knew what I wanted to do. I remember that I liked drawing pictures, I liked art. I got to draw lots of pictures and learned how to paint in high school. I went to college for Media Marketing, because media sounded like drawing pictures, and marketing sounded like money. As it turns out, it was more of a business degree than an art one.

Okay, cool, so now I was into business.

Everyone always said art was for people who didn't like money anyway. I liked money, right? So: less pictures. More charts and graphs and business presentations. Then my favorite professor told me that if I wanted to be super serious about business I might want to consider getting a Masters degree straight out of college, so I did that too. I later found myself holding a Masters degree, an incredible amount of student loan debt, and had completely left the drawings behind.

So I got the grades and I got the diploma. College complete. *Check.* That was a choice I made on my own. I did it. I had accomplished something that put me in a league outside of my parents' influence.

As for Emily and I... well.

"Do you want to be like, a thing?" I asked.

"Yeah." She said.

"I love you." She said.

"I love you, too." I said.

"Do you want to come to Seattle with me?" She asked.

"Yeah." I said.

"People who never leave, never change."

I didn't want to stay in Rochester, and I liked the idea of going back to New Jersey to be near my parents even less. We had a temporary job working for her dad lined up on the Washington-Idaho border, and planned to settle together in Seattle so she could get her own Masters degree. Everything was working out. We packed our things, said our goodbyes, and set off on an adventure with our modest belongings in my tiny blue hatchback, together.

We took three weeks to drive a relaxed and nearly 4,000 mile route through rain and snow and sun and explored middle America. We did touristy things and car-camped to save money. The thing I remembered the most was how big the sky was.

Pause.

I want to describe my favorite feeling in the world.

It's a rare feeling,

one that you can only get when looking out at the ocean,

or deep into a clear and starry night sky,

or at the top of a mountain.

When you can see for miles and miles and miles,

no other human in sight.

No buildings,

no roads.

No mechanical humming or idle chatter.

Just the wind, and you.

That brief moment where you can pretend

you're the only person on the planet, or that

you don't exist at all.

We were driving somewhere in the Badlands in South Dakota,

and I was compelled to stop along the side of the road and step

outside.

I looked out over the vast prairie landscape.

It was perfectly flat and endless.

I'd never seen earth act like seawater.

No one in sight.

Short, soft grass swayed in the air

and stretched all the way to the foggy horizon.

Breathe.

Breathe again.

I turned around, and there was the road, some passing cars, Emily.

Ready to move on.

***

We chose the job with her dad because it was the easy thing to do.

We chose to move into a tiny apartment on the Idaho border because it was the easy thing to do.

We chose to move into a tiny apartment in Seattle because it was the easy thing to do.

I chose a job taking phone calls for a manageable, if unimpressive, paycheck because it was the easy thing to do.

Moving to Seattle meant that I'd have to start all over. The big fish in the small pond became the little fish in the big pond: I was a nobody again. I mean, sure, I took a volunteer gig sweeping floors and ushering guests at a local improv theater to try to stay connected to the community I left behind. But by that point the connection was already severed. I sat in a dusty audience seat, shoulder-to-shoulder with drunk patrons watching other performers soak up the limelight. I swelled with the laughter that filled the room. I cheered the comedians for their brilliance. I hated that I had to watch life move on without me in it. I gave up comedy. After all, I needed to get a real job.

Sorry, it's hard to write about the past without coming across as bitter.

But you know how the story goes: it's not all that different from how most people end up living their life. Emily and I pulled out our checklists and followed them like a roadmap. Emily had her checklist; I had mine. No singular entity wrote these checklists for us, they simply manifested at the same time our names entered the universal conversation. When life becomes bigger and scarier than you think you can handle, the checklist is the easy thing to do. No one judges you for following a script.

Time passed. We had our jobs, our friends, and we had each other. We eyeballed that next big item that was on both of our lists: marriage. And wouldn't you know it, they have a handy checklist for that too.

In the end, everyone's favorite wonder couple managed to pull it off. They chose to get hitched in front of friends and family, in their favorite city, with good jobs, and put the down payment on a house of their very own. They got the keys. They were perfect. They were ready to become human.

[[HAPPILY EVER AFTER]]

Tags: TG, Magical, Unwilling, Rings, Unaware, Sex

"Do you—Lisa—take Jonathan, to be your lawfully wedded husband, in sickness and in health, for richer or for poorer, so long as you both shall live?"

I looked at Jon and smiled my faux smile, still tasting the light lipstick on my carefully painted lips. I had been practicing. He smiled back at me knowingly, and after a brief pause I finally replied.

Jon was my best friend, but not in the sappy kind of way. We'd known each other since we were boys. He even saved my life once, back in college when I threatened to overdose. I had to return the favor.

***

"Hey Ken? Will you pretend to be a girl and fake-marry me in front of my crazy family?" He said to me one day.

"I... What?"

"My parents have been getting on my case about not getting a nice girl in my life since I moved out here. Trust me, I know a really simple spell they wouldn't be able to detect. And you can go back to your normal self after the wedding and count on them never bothering you afterwards."

I owed him though. "Fine, but no tongue when we have to kiss up there. When's the wedding?"

"In two months. I'm going to change you now, though. We need to get started with prep if it's going to work." He flexed his fingers and pointed at me. His eyes glowed with magical energy. Magic didn't come easy to Jon, but I knew it was working when I felt my body gurgle and shift.

"So—so soon??" I whimpered as my rib cage shrank. The weirdest feeling was my hair lengthening out of my head at a quick pace, and my chest inflating. I cupped my new breasts in bewilderment and felt them grow more sensitive the larger they got. All the while, my genitals receded and formed a tight little mound under my pants.

"I don't get to keep my dick!?" I complained.

"Sorry, we need to be convincing, or my family *will* find out. You don't want them to find out..."

I put my hands on my hips and shook my head. "This better be worth the effort, man."

***

"I do." I said.

Jon had carefully hypnotized dozens of strangers, and filled the pews with them as my fake family. I looked over at Jon's mom and she smiled at me.

"Jonathan, do you take Lisa..."

Jon's family was rich with magic. Not every family was so lucky, I couldn't even cast the simplest spells. I caught eye contact with Jon's aunt Gretchen, who was staring at me with profound interest. What I didn't know was that she had made sure that her nephew would be happily married—no matter what.

***

"Can I see the rings, then?" Aunt Gretchen asked Billy, Jon's best man. Billy pulled them from his pocket and let the older woman look at them. They were nothing special, though they had a small spell cast on them to look quite glamorous and expensive. "Oh, they're beautiful!" She exclaimed. "Say, what do you know about this Lisa girl?"

"Supposedly Jon's been seeing her for the past year, but I only heard about her about two months ago. So I'm not sure! She seems nice?"

"Peculiar..." Gretchen thought to herself. "Well, I want Jon to be happy, and I'm sure he wouldn't mind living happily ever after with this girl, she's quite lovely."

"Yeah, she's pretty hot." Billy laughed. "Jon made quite a catch!"

Gretchen rolled her eyes and put her hand over the bride's ring, causing it to glow faintly as she enchanted them. "Cheers to the happy couple!" She smiled.

***

"I do." Jon grinned at me. Ugh. Please let's just get this over with. Though I had to give Jon some credit, this whole ceremony was quite convincing! All the boys on his side of the aisle were checking me out, too, which was at least a sign that the spell he cast on me convinced them, too. There was always a risk we'd be found out.

"May we have the rings?" The officiant gestured to Billy, Jon's best man. He provided the two rings and the officiant gave the first to Jon.

"Jon, as you put this ring on Lisa's finger, repeat after me..."

I curled my lip downward and shuffled in place, my heels getting awfully uncomfortable. I can't believe I agreed to this. I lifted my delicate hand with the freshly painted ruby-colored nails and Jon took it. He positioned the ring in a holding pattern, then recited after the officiant.

I looked at the jewel encrusted ring and thought I saw a brief glimmer of magical green. Raising an eyebrow, but nothing more.

Finally, he slipped the ring on my finger.

I felt... warmer.

I looked down at my new, simply *gorgeous* ring and admired it on my hand. It looked amazing!

"Lisa, your turn." The officiant said, snapping me out of my trance. I looked back at Jon. Jon looked so... handsome in that suit! I blushed a bit, almost tearing up. That earned me a weird look from Jon, but I thought nothing of it.

"Lisa, as you place this ring on Jon's finger, repeat after me..."

I couldn't wait! I slipped the ring on his finger as I recited my lines we practiced earlier that day. We were getting married!!

"...pronounce you, husband and wife. You may kiss the bride!"

Cheers erupted from our families as Jon took me in his arms and kissed me. I felt so light and happy with his warmth and passion, kissing him felt like the most natural thing in the world. I hungered for him, and my tongue slipped through his lips desperate to drink him deeper. This took him by surprise!!

The rest of the world seemed to fade out and I was left with euphoria as I realized what we had done. We were married! We walked down the aisle past our family and friends in linked arms. I couldn't help but kiss him again in front of everyone before we got in the car to our getaway honeymoon.

"Everything alright?" He asked once we got in the car.

"Of course honey, we're married!! I love you soooo much!" I sidled next to him and threw my arms around him to kiss him again. Jon gave me a puzzled and concerned look for some reason, but kissed me anyway. I decided to think nothing of it for now, a wedding is always stressful!

***

"A Happily Ever After spell? Aunt Gretchen, isn't that a bit much?" Jon's mother Frida asked, concerned.

"Nonsense, my dear. We all want Jon to be happy, and he finally picked a girl that he likes enough to marry. I'm ensuring we won't have to pay for a divorce, or worse—a second wedding! I cast it on Lisa's ring, but with enough exposure to her love energy the magic will start to rub off on him, too. They'll be cute little love birds forever." She winked. "And I know you want grandbabies…"

***

I was admiring my beautiful green ring the entire flight to Maui. I couldn't believe it! Me, Mrs. Lancaster! To think that before I was some ordinary boring guy, and now I'm a beautiful princess with a fucking hot husband! Jon stayed quiet during the flight, but I took his hand into mine at every opportunity to remind him how much I loved him.

At the hotel, I quickly dropped my things in a corner of the room and jumped in the shower to freshen up.

"L-Lisa?" I heard Jon say. "Are you sure you're alright, you're acting a little… different." I emerged from the shower after toweling off and posed naked for him.

"Different how, baby? Like I'm your incredible and sexy wife?" I winked.

Jon couldn't stop staring. Good! I broke the ice by approaching him and tugging at his pants to free his lovely dick. If he was gonna play hard-to-get, I suppose I'd have to make the moves for him!

"Lisa, you don't have to..." he started, but I already had his cock in my hand. I looked at him with a *quiet, you* expression and took him into my mouth. He tasted of salt and sweat but I didn't care, I loved him.

He leaned back a bit and guiltily let himself enjoy it. I bobbed my head up and down his cock, wriggling my tongue on his tip to drive him mad! I wanted him so badly...

"I... I love you, too...?" he coughed. I could still sense uncertainty, but that was okay, I loved him anyway! I smiled and climbed on his lap.

"Fuck my pussy, baby, I'm your woman now..." I purred, ready. He looked bewildered, but as he took my hips in his hands I could see his expression changing from doubt to interest. His cock was hard—I made sure of that—and he lowered me onto it. It felt so incredible!

He thrust while I bounced, taking every inch of his dick in me. I never knew! I never knew how great love could feel! He squeezed my ass even harder as we rocked the hotel bed. I squealed and giggled, my mouth hanging open as the feeling of happiness and sex washed over me. As my handsome new husband came.

"Oh shit," he said, somewhat startled, "I'm not wearing a condom!"

I leaned over and kissed him, still gyrating on his dick and taking him in. "We're married now, my love. I don't care."

V

Hunger

TAGS: KAYLA, TG, WILLING

The waters were a lot calmer this evening. Kayla bathed in the false sunlight, adrift on her plank of pornographic tapestry. She wore dark shades and stretched out her long non-legs, kissed a vibrant warmer tone by the sun. Her non-arms gently held the latest story she'd fished from the sea and drank it in as she pondered every sweet word of it. She was relaxed here.

She observed as leaflets appeared from the deck of a passing ship, tossed into the air and scattered to the wind, floating down to the water as paper does. She rescued a sheet mid-air, as other pages fell to either side of her. A sensuous tale of a man who cheated on his wife, and once she found out about it she had him tormented, feminized, and humiliated into acting the role of a submissive housemaid. Kayla felt the hungered bubbling underneath her, the frenzy of the countless lost souls who hadn't scraped together anything to stay afloat. She could see no more than a blur breach the surface and then be gone, a click of water kicking into the air, having devoured the story as food.

Sometimes she'd catch a glimpse of the benefactors on the decks of the great ships. They were as faceless as she was, and no less formless.

Their non-presence was brought to life by their charity to the ghosts below.

Their prose was varied and plentiful. They issued erotic stories of boys transforming into girls, girls transforming into boys, all leaving behind the shackles of their former lives. A lot of it was rewarding to read, and other times it was maddening drivel laden with typos and plot holes. There were professionals and amateurs, good and bad writing, something for every palette. The intention of their charity was pretty clear, to serve their own sexual inclinations or perhaps to challenge their writing skills.

The ghosts didn't care. They would eat anything put in front of them. They were starving. Bottom feeders.

Kayla laughed at the double entendre.

It wasn't lost on her that she was once queen of her own palace, and was now the same as the rest of the ghosts in this endless sea.

She was a small fish. A nobody.

The realization struck her cold; she remembered her pain of not possessing the ability to breach the barrier of touch. Reading these stories wouldn't fix her, and even recognizing that she was not alone in the struggle brought her no comfort.

She looked up at the towering ships. Those ghosts aren't different from me, she told herself, they've just found a way to use those words. She knew how to bend words to make Buddies, so why couldn't she use those same words to capture the attention of an audience?

The shapes of the ghosts swirled beneath her, immeasurable in number. Perhaps they've all come to the ocean for the same reasons she had.

She was nothing in these waters. Even the porn she allowed to pass through her hands swirled and mixed in with the rest of the hungry ghosts here. She could feel the impermanence of it all. How pointless it was to exist among them with no firm ground to stand on. Not like the ship captains. They had it all.

They were the ones who built the oceans, she surmised. In their charity they filled the seas with their visions, these endless waters that kept the ghosts fed. Their ships were made of their efforts. This gave them permanence, history, legacy.

She had permanence once, when she kept her soul intact. When she told people her name. When she danced as an illusion among the living with a borrowed body. When she listened to their music and laughed at their jokes as though she had ears and a heart of her own.

If Kayla couldn't have a body, perhaps she could build a ship.

She tried not to think about where she came from, the events that lent to her situation as a castaway in an endless sea of pornography. She tried not to think about how she had betrayed James's trust. Or what that meant about her character.

Oh, to be human! It was cruel that humanity was only offered as a fantasy. Sometimes she dreamed that she was a boy, a normal boy, absent of her history and her troubles. A normal person moving about a normal world. She got angry, resentful feelings swelling within her. A taste of thunder roared in the distance.

Deep breath in, deep breath out. It wasn't her fault she couldn't have these things. If she could have had a different life, any life, she would have. She was doing the best she could with what she had.

She knew she'd never become human, so why was she fighting so hard?

She got mad again.

What greater being existed in this place that would stop her from realizing her potential? What right did it have to prevent her—or any of the other ghosts dancing in the depths—from becoming real? The ships are as fake as anything else in this world of words and sex and sadness.

Frustration burning into determination, she reached into the cold waters and pulled up a photo of a topless woman. Her hair was a tousled dirty blonde, but still camera ready. She had a solemn look on her face, one side of her lip bitten under pearly teeth, a flush of color on her cheeks. She stares at the camera lens. Unsure. But nonetheless carefully posed. Carefully, Kayla spun a tale about a boy being turned into a girl against his will. Same as the others she had read, but better. This one was hers.

She tied the girl to that brick of text, and reshaped it into a plank of wood and words. It would make a sturdy enhancement to her modest raft. She carved a suitable title into it, *"Mind Games."* Her first of many.

She pulled copies from the fibers of the wood, gathering them like leaflets in her non-arms until she had the courage to share. In one motion, she flicked her non-wrist and flung the story into the ocean.

The ghosts caught the scent, and bobbed up to the surface for their meal. Kayla looked into the filthy murk below, and watched as the ghosts feasted gleefully on her words. They gurgled and burped and asked for more.

I'm so glad you like it. She smiled, and started working on the next one.

[[MIND GAMES]]

TAGS: TG, REMOTE, MAGICAL, UNWILLING

"Nothing happened." The girl looked upset at the man holding the remote. "Why aren't you changing me back into a man?"

Mark laughed a little, continuing to examine the remote's manual. "Maybe it's because you've always been a girl, '*Steph anie*.'"

"Don't try to fuck with me like that, Mark. Your mind games don't work and it creeps me out that you're even trying."

Steven would be trying to change himself back, but Mark had found a mind control setting that convinced him the remote could only transform other people. Steven was powerless to do anything about it, and Mark wanted to try and convince the new girl to accept her new reality without cheating with the remote... too much.

"Here, I think I found something that would help." Mark typed something into the remote's keypad. "How do you feel now?"

"Nothing happened again. I'm still a girl! The remote clearly isn't working." She looked disappointed. "I thought it would have been fun to try being a man, even for a little while."

"Yeah, I guess the thing's busted, or maybe it's a scam." Mark smiled at Stephanie.

"Oh well, whatever babe, I don't believe in magic remotes anyway. Did you want to get a quickie in before we go to meet your parents?"

"I'd love to."

WRITING

TAGS: THE AUTHOR, MAGICAL, WILLING, WRITING, SEX

"I'm going to cum inside you. I'm going to finish what the spell started. You will be a girl forever!"

The moon reflected off the water. A symphony of creaks and groans escaped the muscles of the boats outside my cabin, all sleeping on the night's gentle waves.

I found myself here. Tucked into a sleeping bag in the upper portion of a bunk bed in the tiny living quarters on Emily's parents' family boat. I could hear Emily's soft breathing in the lower bunk. She was fast asleep, like everyone else. The boat rocking in the calm water made sure of that. I had stayed up a little too late reading through erotic stories online.

Now that I was married, my opportunities for alone time were a little more scarce. I had to take the moments I could get, and this sleeping quarters was small enough that I could get my own bunk instead of sleeping curled like wires around Emily.

I scrolled through story after story. Reading the same beats over and over again.

He spread her legs wide and inserted his throbbing member into her warm and eager pussy.

It had been like this for some time. Occasionally closing the door to my world and retreating into these situations so I could feed. I snuck some tissues into a corner of the bed ahead of time, in case I needed them. I needed them. I knew I'd do this to myself. I was disgusting.

This place in my mind was where my muse lived, and this was the journey I had to take to meet it. Touching myself allowed me to reach a spot that no one else could, it was a wellspring. My body entered such a state of euphoria. Words bubbled up as light as air from my soul and spilled onto a page. I didn't choose these words, these were simply the words that existed in me. I released them to ease the pain building in a corner of my chest.

I read a story of a man losing a bet, the penalty being transformed into a curvaceous girl. The story goes on and the new girl loses yet another bet, and has to fuck the man she lost to. The story goes on to her losing yet another bet, and she has to become his wife, his submissive sex slave.

I had never written a sex scene. It felt wrong. I knew how much Emily hated porn. How it objectified women and girls. How it infantilized them, devalued them, pitted them against one another. And here I was, palm milky on a hot phone writing porn not three feet away from my sleeping wife in the darkness.

She got on her knees and saw his cock for the first time. She'd seen her own, of course, but she's never seen one from... this angle.

144

What if I was bad at it? Was this weird? Why am I doing this, anyway?

[[Doesn't this feel good? Don't you want to fall into the black hole of your sexual cravings, and give in completely. Touch it, massage it, live inside its wetness, fucking *destroy* it?]]

I scrolled through some images to keep the inspiration flowing. Keep the wellspring hot. My autopilot engaged. I saw a brunette. She's on her knees, in a tight black tank, no bra, hands combing up through her wavy hair to display it high over her head. She's looking down and to the side, playing at being bashful. Eyes mostly but not quite closed. She's got that cat-eye eyeliner look, with wings that can cut. She's a bad girl, she wants it bad. So bad. So fucking bad. I swiped over to the Notes app and started writing.

She leaned in and took his cock into her lips. Feeling its alien curves, density, weight. She'd never had anything like this in her mouth before. She'd never tasted anything like this. She wasn't sure what to do.

I'd never given a blowjob before, much less ever wanted to give one. After all, I'm a straight man. I was born that way. But this felt good to write, trying to put myself in a novice's position. Imagining myself on my knees, imagining the events as I commanded them. Warm. Excited. Eager. Pampered. I could feel my body respond to every word I typed. I didn't want it to stop, so I edged myself and didn't allow myself to cum just yet. I allowed my brain to travel for a moment to pretend that my dick was something else.

Stop. That's weird.

"Get on the bed. I want to fuck you." He said. Oh no, what's that going to be like?

What *is* that going to be like? I can write whatever I want. I'm in control. I'm the master.

[[And the servant.]]

I'm the boy.

[[And the girl.]]

I felt his rock-hard cock enter my pussy. I felt its presence echo throughout my body. Its shape, its texture. His musculature pressing against my soft skin. It pressed in and pulled out, in and out. I was being fucked. I cried out in small whimpers and sharp breaths. It hurt.

I think it hurt? I didn't know, [[but I wanted to.]]

[[I wanted to know what it was like.]]

Magical, Unwilling

Tags: TG, Kayla, Writing

Kayla felt warmth. The kind of warmth one might experience after a healthy morning jog, or the residual heat one carries with them after a full day of sunbathing. She wiped the sweat from her non-brow, and kept working.

Kayla didn't know how to build a boat. She pasted it together with the scraps of emotions and the glue of phrases she was able to pull into form. She didn't understand words like keel, or bow, or stem, rib or frame, treenails or trunnels, caulking or galleys or hatches. Instead she guided her non-hands to do the work of assembling the ship over the water as she willed it, with the language of those ghosts adrift beneath her.

With effort, her raft had grown into a small boat. It lacked the polish of those larger ships, but every nail and plank was hammered into place with increasing conviction. Nothing was wasted. In a moment of rest she crossed her non-arms over the rail of her non-wooden vessel, and peered over the edge, down into the deep dark again.

She was a writer now, and with this new vantage point on her small craft she could see what the ghosts wanted and how they fed. She knew the currents that brought them to this unquiet sea. She knew their proclivities. How hungry they were for change, to be freed from the cold water. These ghosts had developed a thirst for fantasies of the most incredible transformation of all.

Magical / Willing

The pressure in the room drops as cosmic energy pours from a simple brass lamp, once rubbed. A being of unimaginable beauty spills out in a cloud of purple smoke, their hair floating like jellyfish tendrils, their body perfect and glowing. They speak effortlessly, and with command. "I am the genie of this lamp, young master, and I shall grant you three wishes."

"Anything I want?" The boy clutching the lamp, shaking, already knows what he wants. He's afraid to sound too eager.

"Anything." The genie is patience.

"Well, then. I wish I was a girl."

Magical/Willing stories focus on magical transformations where the transformed person is completely aware and can provide consent to be changed. These are frequently optimistic stories that allow the reader to believe they can be anything they want to be. Perhaps they can drink a potion and be instantly transformed into a person of the opposite gender. Or it's a story about a person with the power to shapeshift at will. These are adventurous stories, explorations of fun that put the agency into the transformed person's hands. They *want* this change, and have done the emotional processing of what it means to be transformed. These are for the people who want to push a magic button, and instantly be transformed into the opposite gender.

Kayla found these stories unsatisfying, they made for weak materials.

Realistic / Willing

The girl, alone in her room, spins in front of a mirror. She feels the fabric of the new dress tickle against her freshly shaved legs as it swishes. Her makeup is caked on a little too heavily, but she's still learning. She grabs a hairbrush and starts to brush through her still-too-short hair. It'll grow out.

The knock-knocking on the door startles her. "Michael? Michael, are you in there?"

Shit, she wasn't supposed to get home yet. She thinks about answering but her voice catches in her throat. Better to run. Far, far better to run. She slips open her bedroom window, and slinks out into the tree line behind their house, still wearing her mother's new peach-colored heels.

Realistic/Willing stories focus on realistic transformations that occur to a willing participant. The narrative may present obstacles for the transformed parties that may be keeping them from getting the transformation they want, since realistic transformations involve real-world technologies. It may be a matter of access, or permissions from others, that drive the conflict in the story. The transformed person has all the agency, and acts as a role model for readers that might be looking for a more optimistic outcome for gender transition.

These stories may be popular with people who have already done some emotional processing and are looking for stories that validate their own lived experiences in getting the transformation they want for themselves.

This also had little value to Kayla. This wasn't what her ghosts craved.

Realistic / Unwilling

"What... what happened to me?" The girl said, groggy, waking up after hours of bed rest.

"Good, you're awake." A strange man in a pristine white coat stood over the girl's hospital bed. "You'll find that we made some enhancements."

"En-enhancements?" The girl stammered. Her voice caught, and she ran her hand across her neck. She was very bandaged, and she felt the pain everywhere. Her body felt fundamentally altered.

"Yes, after your accident left you incapacitated, you received a full suite of improvements. This came at the request of your husband, Don."

"My...husband?" The girl hardly had consciousness enough to process what was happening. Perhaps she was dreaming. Don wasn't her husband, Don wanted her dead. Her? Wasn't she a... But she was so tired, her eyes fluttered closed again.

Realistic/Unwilling stories focus on realistic transformations where the transformed person is subjected to the change without their consent. These are generally dark and ethically corrupt stories. Maybe a person has been in some kind of accident, and doctors decide the only way to recover the patient is to perform surgeries that would dramatically alter the person's appearance. Or perhaps it's a revenge plot, and the person is humiliated, kidnapped, tortured, or tricked into engaging in hormone replacement therapy and undergoes a gender transformation that way. "Realistic" is a stretch, though some other writers try to push the envelope on what could reasonably happen with the technology and motives of people in the real world, without dipping into fantasy tools. These are usually the outcomes of nefarious schemes by twisted parties, the transformed person does not *want* the change and does not need to do any of the emotional processing to consider the ramifications of their transformation.

Magical / Unwilling

Ah, yes. This was the stuff that enriched the sea, riled the emotions of the creatures below, stirred them to frenzy. Fantastical transformations that happen to people who don't want them.

Victims are subjected to grotesque transformations and sexual scenarios against their will that teeter around ethics and consent. People who enjoy this type of content are navigating complex emotions.

Magical / Unwilling transformations allow the reader to be as far removed from reality as it gets. The ultimate escapist fantasy. The transformation could never happen in real life, and the victim never has to make an informed decision that they *want* this transformation in the first place. They have no agency, and are never expected to do the hard emotional work to consider the ramifications of making the changes for themselves.

Often, stories like this end in complete and total erasure of the transformed person's former identity. Perhaps they forget they were *ever* a man, or are subjected to even crueler forms of erasure—like being self-aware and locked inside of a body they no longer have any control over. Perhaps they are put into a position where they have no choice but to go along with the change, with no hope of turning back, and are subjected to humiliation for a change they didn't ask for.

This was the blood that came beating from Kayla's non-heart. These were the words that escaped when she cut open to the world.

[[CHANGE OF HEART]]

TAGS: TG, MAGICAL, UNWILLING, SPELL, MENTAL
CHANGES, TRICKED, SEX

Cry and complain. That's all he did for like, three days. The spell we ended up casting accidentally caused Mike to turn into a beautiful young woman, not the macho muscled hunk he wanted to be.

"You need to fix this!!" He shouted, wrapping his much smaller body with a blanket so we couldn't look at what he'd become. He shut himself in his bedroom, slamming the door behind him.

Of course, Roger and I tried to find a counterspell. Something to undo it, but I was starting to think it didn't exist. We'd have to find another way.

One night, I had a twisted thought. What if I couldn't fix him? He'd be terribly upset for the rest of his—or her—life! I browsed the book for something different. A way to change his mind about it.

"Can I come in?" I asked, tapping on the door lightly. I heard him stir and open the door, his cute little girl face peeking out, tears still dry on her rosy cheeks.

"What do you want, Pete... it's late. Did you find the cure?" He asked, meekly.

I nodded, and Mike allowed me in the room. It was mostly trashed, holes in the walls, cabinets asunder. He was a wreck.

"Okay, but this had better work." He sat on the bed, cross legged and covered in that blanket. I pulled out the book and sat across from him. Was I actually doing this to Mike? What would Roger think? Shaking my head, I knew I had to press on. This was for Mike's benefit.

"Xaster Remularis, Tikalum Gemorika!"

When I read the words, Mike's head whipped back, then faced forward again. His eyes were glazed over. He just... sat there, saying nothing.

I waved a hand in front of his face... nothing. "Okay, um..." I thought. I didn't actually think this far ahead, I realized. "What is your name?"

"My name is Michael Shaun Reading," he responded, plain as day.

"No, that's not right. Your name is Michelle Samantha Reading." I gulped.

"My name is Michelle Samantha Reading." He replied again as confidently as before.

Oh, it actually worked. I paused, staring at the unblinking girl in front of me and pressed on.

"W-why are you a woman?"

"We tried to make me more masculine using the magic book, but the spell we found was wrong. It turned me into a girl by mistake, and I am trying to become a man again."

I needed to be clever. "That's not right. You... wanted to be turned into a girl, so you intentionally swapped the spells on us. We cast the feminizing spell on you so you could live your dream of being a girl."

Her eyes remained glazed over and emotionless. I decided to double down.

"You always wanted to be a girl. Now, you are one. Roger still thinks you want to be a man, but that's okay to you. If you keep up this charade a little longer, he'll think you've finally accepted being a woman."

The blanket she was wearing started falling off her slender shoulders, as she continued to stare into space. She was still wearing her old, ragged men's button-down, no bra.

"You... wanted to be a pretty, sexy girl. Someone who could wear beautiful women's clothing with pride. You also..." I was getting too excited about this. But there was no turning back at this point. "...always wanted to be with me. But you knew I'd never love you as a man. And now, finally, as a woman, you can have me."

Her eyes regained their focus as the spell ended. She looked around the room before returning her gaze to me. "Peter, when do you think I can stop pretending? I never want to be a man again!" She fully removed the blanket and stretched, her bosom thinly veiled by the shirt she was wearing. "I just want to act like my true self..."

"I uh..." I stared. Fuck, she was gorgeous. The way she talked had changed dramatically. Her voice oozed femininity, like she was a girl this whole time.

"I can't stand wearing these men's clothes anymore, can you help me buy some proper bras and panties tomorrow morning?" She asked in a huff, removing her shirt entirely. Her perfect tits were bared for me. Seeing me staring, she giggled. "Oh Pete, baby, I'm glad we're finally alone together..." She dropped her sweatpants, proudly revealing her magnificence.

It was 3 in the morning. Roger was definitely asleep. He couldn't hear us as I approached the nubile woman in front of me, touched her and kissed her. She removed my belt hungrily seeking my manhood, and we faded into a horny mess of flesh and lust.

***

"Hey, Pete?" Roger asked me a few days later. "Has Mike been acting... weird?"

"Huh?" I knew Roger would start noticing something was off. After all, Michelle had started wearing the bra and panty sets I bought for her, and had a certain affinity for short feminine dresses. "Er, maybe she—uh, he, is getting more comfortable with his new body?"

Roger looked concerned. "We still haven't found the counterspell for him. And frankly, have you even been trying to find one?"

"We've looked everywhere, man! Besides, maybe we should be happy for Mike..." I looked over at Mike's bedroom door, behind which I knew a buxom girl was currently humming, admiring herself in the mirror while she modeled her new lingerie. "He seems happier."

The door opened, and Michelle emerged.

She was wearing a tight dress, and her hair looked remarkable. She posed dramatically, showing off in the doorway, "Oh, hey boys," she said before walking into the kitchen to grab a glass of water. She looked at me, and winked.

Roger swallowed hard. I couldn't blame him, Michelle oozed sex appeal now. I knew he'd be confused and conflicted seeing his old wrestling buddy proudly wearing a dress and heels. "Are you sure you're okay, Mike? I thought you hated it."

"You know," she started, "I'm feeling sooo much better. I feel like I'm finally getting the hang of this 'girl' thing, you know? Like maybe I can relax and try it for a while?" She leaned on the countertop, her soft breasts pushing outward, curtained by the loose fabric of the dress. Her eyes kept meeting mine.

"Oh, Pete, that reminds me..." she said before taking a swig of her water, "can you help me in my room for a minute?"

Cut to four minutes later, and her TV is blaring to drown out the sounds of her riding my cock. Her tits jiggle as she thrusts herself back and forth, driving my dick deep in her wet and wanting pussy. My hands grip her hips as she gyrates her pelvis, taking in the intensity as best as she can.

This isn't like the first night, though. The night where I cast the spell to make Mike believe that he wanted this. The first night was her first time getting fucked by a man. This is now her third, and by now she knows what she wants. I know she has started craving it, and since she is 'free' to behave like a girl in front of me she's not ashamed to ask me to slap her ass and caress her tits to make her cry out in pleasure. She repeats my name hungrily between careful and soft moans, trying half-heartedly not to have Roger overhear us.

I can't get enough of her. After several glorious minutes my body stiffens as I release my cum into her shiny, new, tight, near-virginal core.

"Mmm, Petey. That was wonderful." She coos, her hair splayed out on the pillow next to me as she entangles her newly shaven legs against mine. "I love the way you make me feel. I love being a girl. Let's never talk about me ever being a gross boy ever again."

"But what about Roger..." I start. She places two fingers on my lips.

"What if Roger doesn't have to know? We have a spellbook, right? I'm sure there's a way to make him see things different-ly..."

She had that look in her eye that screamed both "I'm being naughty" and "let's fuck again."

***

I was on top of the world, and my cock was getting pretty sore. Michelle was my sex goddess. She reveled in her femininity and was starting to care less and less about 'pretending' to want to turn back into a man around Roger.

But, one day, when I wasn't home...

"Mike, you seem different. Are you sure the spell we cast on you isn't affecting your mind?" Roger asked, as Michelle brought back two shopping bags full of women's apparel. She was wearing a hot pink top and tiny jean shorts, with incredible heels to match the outfit. That, and she was wearing a full face of makeup.

Definitely not the behavior from a guy-accidentally-turned-girl-that-for- all-reasonable-expec-tations-should-want-to-be-a-man-again.

She huffed. "Roger, I would prefer it if you called me by my real name, Michelle. I don't know where you got the idea in your head that my name is Mike, even if I used to be a..." she coughed on her words, and flipped her hair, "...you know."

"Okay, that's it. Something is wrong with you!" Roger exclaimed. "We need to fix it, now."

Before Roger could stand up, though, Michelle grinned. **"Xaster Remularis, Tikalum Gemorika!"**

Roger's eyes clouded over, and he sat motionless and quiet on the couch in a trance.

"Huh, can't believe that worked." Michelle mused to herself, happy that the spell she read in my spellbook could be used as a convincing mechanism and erase all doubts in Roger's mind about her woman-ness.

"Let's try this, shall we?" Michelle sat with one leg crossed over the other. "Roger, do you know who I am?"

"You are Michael Shaun Reading. You are my roommate and best bud."

Michelle scrunched her face disappointedly. "No, that's wrong! I'm Michelle Samantha Reading, you should have known that by now."

"Of course, you are Michelle Samantha Reading." Roger replied, matter-of-factly.

Satisfied, Michelle pressed on. "Do you know how I became a girl?"

"Yes, the three of us accidentally cast a spell to make you a woman. We have been trying hard for the past week to change you back into a man."

Frustrated again, Michelle gripped the edge of her chair. "No, no! I don't want to be a man again... I don't..." She gathered herself, and came up with a brilliant and naughty idea.

"No, I've never been a man. I have always been a girl! You know me as Pete's girlfriend, but we can still be friends."

"You are Pete's girlfriend, Michelle."

Michelle giggled. This was too much fun. She admired Roger's cloudy eyes and saw that she could still play with him. She thought about how much it hurt her to think that Roger wanted her to be a man again. Why would anyone want that, when they could be free, when they could be themselves?

"You're jealous." She started.

"Jealous of who?" Roger asked.

"Jealous of me. You want to be pretty." Michelle stripped off her shorts and panties, fully exposing herself to the entranced man. She wanted him to idolize her body.

"You want to be like me, but you can't be like me, because you're a silly man. You hide it, of course, but deep down you want to be a girl. You want to be changed into a girl. You want to know what it feels like so badly you can't stand it. I'm also the only person you trust to tell your secret to."

"I want to be a girl." Roger replied.

Satisfied, Michelle pulled her clothes back on. "Good boy, now wake." She snapped her fingers and Roger's eyes lost their fog.

He looked around like he lost something else. "Michelle... hi. Sorry, what were we talking about?"

Michelle smiled wide hearing her name said so confidently, "Oh, not much. Just gossiping. You were saying you had something to confess to me?"

Roger blinked. "Oh, um, yes. It's a little personal..." He swallowed, bearing himself for what he was about to admit. He never thought he'd ever tell anyone about his deepest, most true desire. "I want to... become a girl. I want to be a pretty, beautiful girl." He sat back in his seat, embarrassed. "Like you..."

Michelle feigned surprise, but leaned forward in support. "Oh honey, I think there's a spell to help you with exactly that problem."

Roger nodded with caution, but his insides reeled in excitement.

"Finally," he thought to himself.

***

"Are you sure about this?" Michelle asked, hardly able to contain her smile. Roger was standing, awkward and naked, on the sigil they had crudely drawn in chalk on the floor.

Roger covered his penis with his hands. He felt shame over it, though he couldn't quite remember how long he'd felt that shame. Or why he wanted to be a girl so badly. He knew it in his heart that this was right.

He had no clue that Michelle's spell tricked him into thinking it was what he wanted. Or that Michelle had also drawn in an extra rune on the floor that would change his personality even further.

Roger nodded. "Yes..."

Michelle recited the words, and as the sigil started to glow, that was when I walked in.

"Hi guys... wha—" my eyes were drawn to a naked Roger, now glowing in the middle of the room, and Michelle flashing me a wicked smile to greet me. Roger's eyes were shining, as the spell's effects took hold of him.

"What did you do!?" I yelled.

"He and I didn't see eye to eye about me being a girl. So I wanted to give him a chance at a change of heart!" She beamed. Meanwhile, Roger's hair burst from his scalp, and his torso started to morph.

"I don't... how? Why?" I stared slackjaw at Roger's transformation. He couldn't have done this willingly. Michelle was up to something...

"I learned a trick! And now, with Roger out of the way, there's nothing to stop me from being the woman I was always meant to be, baby." She sidled up to me, her warm breath on my neck, her gentle hand gliding down my pants.

"No, this is... this is different." I said, the feeling of her fingers arousing and scaring me as I witnessed Roger lose himself inch by inch. Thinking back on hypnotizing Mike to make him believe he wanted to be a girl, I realized that I made a terrible mistake. "We have to stop this!"

"It's too late, my love. But I can make you see things my way, that it's better this way."

Michelle kissed me, then whispered in my ear.

"Xaster Remularis, Tikalum Gemorika!"

My eyes glazed over. The world felt like it was moving in slow motion. I could still see Roger changing, and I became acutely aware of everything and nothing at the same time. Roger's face melted away, only to be reborn in the shape of a lovely young woman's face. Pretty, kissable lips, gorgeous eyes, defined cheekbones.

It didn't matter to me at the moment. I didn't feel like moving, or feeling, or expressing my anger towards Michelle for trapping me like this. For betraying Roger by turning him into a girl as well. Is that what she was about to do to me? I didn't care.

Michelle's lips started moving. She was talking to me. I was unable to hear her words, but felt compelled to answer her.

"You are my girlfriend, Michelle. I am your loyal boyfriend. I'll do anything you want me to do for you." I said.

"You have always been a hot, flirty, sexy girl. I don't remember a time when you weren't." I said.

"Regina is our roommate. She has always been a girl. She's a naughty girl, and deserves everything that comes for her. She is our mutual love pet." I said.

I heard Michelle snap her fingers as I woke up from my daydream. I was a little disoriented at first, but seeing my hot girlfriend smiling at me grounded me in reality again.

"Hey babe, why were you and Regina playing with magic sigils again?"

Michelle pushed me into a chair and climbed on my lap and kissed me. "Oh just trying to make our tits bigger, isn't that right, Regina?"

Regina stood quietly, the faint glow from the sigil finally dissipating. She looked at her body and ran her hands across her chest, feeling the curves of her bosom for the first time. She smiled wickedly, her hand running down her front to explore herself. "Mmmm, yes Michelle, it's wonderful!"

"Regina, you may only refer to me as your mistress." Michelle snapped on her. Regina looked confused, then ashamed as the command sank in.

"Y-yes mistress." She stammered.

"Good. You need to understand your place in this household. You serve your master and mistress." Michelle turned and winked at me. I loved the way my girl took command.

"Yes mistress." Regina replied, more obediently. "I will serve you and master however you like."

Michelle looked at me with a spark of inspiration in her eyes. "I'm feeling generous. You will prepare Pete with a delicious blowjob."

I perked up at this. The new and naked brunette turned her head to look at me, and approached with timid footsteps. Michelle climbed off my lap and watched as Regina knelt before me and pulled my already stiff cock from my pants.

In one last burst of defiance, Regina pleaded. "B-but I've never sucked a man's cock before..."

I felt compelled to instruct her. She was our servant, I reminded myself, she deserved this. I leaned back, and uttered, "You will do as you are told."

With that, Regina could resist no more. She dipped her mouth over the edge of my shaft and closed her eyes as she sucked me off. She wasn't very good at first, but with commands from Michelle she improved quickly. She even began to enjoy herself.

Michelle knelt behind the cocksucking girl and started to stroke Regina's pussy. Regina whimpered at first, but the overwhelming state of arousal had her licking me with even more determination.

"You're a bad girl, Regina." I whispered. "You're such a fucking slut..." My words carried power. Regina's body started moving like a pornstar that had been sucking off boys like me for years. She felt no more fear or shame, she now wore a proud expression of lust and confidence.

My dick twitched as Regina bobbed and gasped in her hunger. I couldn't take it anymore. I groaned and gripped the chair and came right into her mouth, the cum spilling out the sides or her lips as she tried to drink it all up.

I turned to look at Michelle, who was furiously rubbing her own clit in arousal. "Mm, Regina, you're not done yet. Come, tend to me." She said, spreading her legs.

I loved how my girlfriend took control. She was always in control. Seeing our love pet crawl willfully on her knees to lap up Michelle's clit with her cum-soaked tongue made me even more excited for our future together.

Tonight was going to be a long night.

VI

why am I like this

PHONE

TAGS: THE AUTHOR, PHONE, WRITING, WILLING

As soon as my eyes were open, I held my phone to check the responses I had gotten on *Change of Heart*. I refreshed the page, getting another like here, another like there. I watched in the dawn hour as the number trickled upwards to 100, much more than a lot of the other writers were getting. I re-read the comments below the fold.

> **Abigail82** Wow, that was so fucking hot.
>
> **Cumbot69** You should write more!
>
> **Justaduck** Do you take requests, you're incredible!

People—real people!—were reading my work.

I wanted to tell Emily. I wanted to tell my friends. I wanted to post something, *anything*, to social media.

"Look at this thing I made! So many people liked it, they're reading it!"

"Wow! This is so good!" They'd say. *"I had no idea you were such a great writer."* They'd say.

They'd appreciate the effort I put into crafting a cohesive story. They'd appreciate the little twists I'd painstakingly insert. People liked to read erotica, right? This was normal, right?

I'd blush a little and say *"It's only my first one. It wasn't that good..."*

And they'd say *"You don't have to be great to start. But you have to start to be great."* Or something equally profound. But no one was going to say that to me.

I waited, awake, watching Emily experience a perfectly normal morning. Stirring at first, then rolling over to the comfort of her partner, sitting up, and stretching her way out of bed.

"It's such a nice day out! We should go to the park."

My phone held a special kind of cursed serotonin game. I could experience success and recognition so long as I didn't talk about it. The more I played, the greater the potential for an explosive downfall. I couldn't tell Emily, or anyone. It was me, my words, and the likes.

As soon as I had a moment to spare I brainstormed my next story. I was hooked into the game now. Can I get more likes than before? How many different stories can I tell?

I published several short stories that first year. *New You Processing Chamber, Wishes From A Coin, Happily Ever After.* Established myself as someone capable of cranking out content like some of the more recognized TG fiction authors in this community. I wanted to show them that I was different. I wanted my art to rise above the rest.

I needed to be a not-so-anonymous person that could publish content that would exist on the Internet forever. An artist whose work people could truly connect with. A person with staying power. She wouldn't vanish at the end of an Omegle chat log or block you or delete her account when she was discovered. She was an author with an authentic sense of humor. A *real* girl. You could talk to her in the comments section. I took on her personality. I gave her a name: Kayla.

In the end, obviously, none of this mattered. I'd write my story in bed, on the couch, on the toilet, at work, on the airplane, in the hotel room. I'd publish it online. I'd watch the likes trickle in.

But when I shut off my phone, I was shut off from Kayla.

***

I handled my phone in my pocket like it would fall through the seams of my jeans and into public view if I wasn't careful. Today I had set aside some time to step into the small pink building dotted with marketing posters and big smiling faces of people looking at expensive new cell phones.

"Hello, sir. Can I help you with anything?"

"I'm looking to upgrade my phone." I pulled it from my pocket. "I think I'm due for one."

Ugh, maybe I should have cleaned my phone case before turning this in. I had masturbated with it in my hand earlier that day. It must have been too gross to turn in. Surely the customer service agents handled gross phones like this all the time. They probably wash their hands afterwards. Probably.

"Great! We can do that. What kind of phone do you have in mind?"

"Well," I thought about the fact that I wrote porn on my phone, that I scrolled through hundreds of beautiful women a day, that I essentially only ever visited three websites in private mode. "I do everything on my phone. I'll take that one." The one with the biggest screen.

I made sure to close all the browsers open on my phone before handing it over to the salesperson. "Did you want to transfer your photos? You have a lot here, probably photos of you and your wife, right?"

I hoped that he wouldn't pull up the photo app, I wasn't sure what embarrassing photos were saved there last. The things that might expose my inexcusable nature.

"Yeah."

"It'll be about an hour. You can go get lunch if you'd like."

An hour. Okay, that was easy. I shrugged off the anxiety and left the store empty-handed. There was a MOD Pizza next door, so I figured that would be a good place to burn some time. I waited in line behind a family with three small children. The mom told one of them to cut it out. The dad was on his phone, not bothering to look up when the line shifted forward and taking a step to stay in the same small zone as his family. The black-haired girl behind me had lots of witchy tattoos, crows and moons and pentagrams and the like. She looked so cool. She wasn't looking at me.

"What can I get for you, my guy?" The kid behind the counter repeats himself. Regular-sized pie. Lots of spicy toppings. I shuffled over to the soda fountain and grabbed a Coke. Regular. I sipped while I waited, and watched the line of people coming in and ordering pizzas and waiting for the pizzas while tapping the screen on their phones. I wondered what they were reading.

I wondered if any of them read my stories.

Or if any of them had anything to hide.

"It's Katie." I overhear. The girl with the witchy tattoos. She's cute. She's paying for her pizza.

***

"I'm loving this song!" Emily said, later that evening while I was driving us both home. "Do you mind if I check out the lyrics?" She had a habit of keeping her own phone tucked away to limit her time online, unlike me. Seeing my phone stashed into the cup holder, plugged in and playing music on my car speaker, she reached for my phone to pull up a web browser.

No. Stop. Survival instincts kick in. *No.* The hair on the back of my neck stiffened. My pulse quickened as my nervous system was shaken awake. *No!*

Don't touch it.

DON'T

TOUCH

MY

PHONE

I snatched my phone before she could get to it, one hand on the steering wheel, one eye on the road, one eye on the phone. I angled the phone to ensure she couldn't see the screen, opened the web browser and sighed—it wasn't in private mode.

I didn't have an excuse or a lie, and she—for whatever reason—didn't press me on my stunt. I just handed it to her with the browser app open, calculating that she didn't know how to check private mode anyway.

Don't touch my phone, I wanted to say.

Instead I said, "Here you go. It is a pretty good song."

Don't touch my fucking phone.

[[I don't want you to know who I am.]]

This thing will ruin us.

[[I don't want to know who I am.]]

***

"You want to join me and get ready for bed?" Emily called from the bedroom.

"Yeah, yeah, in a minute." I was sitting on the couch, scrolling.

Naked women. Panty shots. Pretty dresses. Makeup. Sissy stories. Sex.

I heard the buzzing of an electric toothbrush from the other room.

I started reading about a guy hypnotized with a magic pocket watch into becoming a female sex slave with gigantic breasts. I scroll past it—that's a bit too much for me. More naked women. Fashion posts.

"Are you coming to bed?" Now she sounded annoyed.

"Yeah, sorry, just finishing something." No I wasn't.

I heard the buzzing of her vibrator coming from the bedroom. Faint gasps and whimpers. I don't think about it. I found a story I actually liked, but it was pretty long. I got up to finally go to the bedroom but realized she's in there, masturbating. It would be rude to interrupt; besides, the door was locked.

I went to the bathroom to sit on the toilet with my phone. Somewhere along the way I decided to read the story.

It was good. Really well written. I admired the author's use of imagery and fantastic realism. My dick is right there, so I jerk off; I didn't last long but I hung out on the toilet anyway, enjoying the story. This guy turns into a girl and gets what he has coming to him. I reveled in his agony, his forced submission.

I felt gross, but it was a feeling. I hit the little *Like* button and watched the count go up by 1.

I looked at the time. Shit, I haven't brushed my teeth. Oh well. I washed my hands, and crawled into bed next to her. She's already snoring. I didn't cuddle next to her—instead, I placed my phone on my nightstand and took what covers I could get.

[[HIS KATIE]]

TAGS: TG, MAGICAL, UNWILLING, WITCH, SPELL, SEX

"Alright class, as many of you may know, I prefer to teach by example. So, in the spirit of that, I'm going to select one student to cast the love spell upon. For educational purposes, of course."

The professor let her eyes drift around the room, settling on me. Her gaze lingered as I sweat a little, then she pointed. Oh shit. "You, girl, what's your name?"

Let's rewind a minute. My name is Brandon, and I'm not actually a girl. I infiltrated a girl's witchcraft school on a dare from my classmates. Yeah, a girl's school.

I have this witch friend, you see, and she said she could get me in to take a class or two before anyone found out, and, well, she had to turn me into a girl to do it. It was a girl's school, after all.

I figured I would enroll in this class on charms and seduction, because I thought it would be funny and my friend said that even as a non-magic user I might be able to do something with it.

I never expected to have any other spell cast on me, and definitely not while looking like this...

"Uh, Katie?" I gulped. The other girls laughed.

"How do you like boys, Katie?"

I answered nervously, I didn't want to blow my cover. "Uhh, they're okay, I guess?"

The professor lifted her hands and whipped them in a flick at me. A shock of light burst from her fingers and it was over. Gasps rang through the room, all eyes on me. I looked at my hands and ran them through my hair, patting myself down. Nothing had changed. I didn't feel any different, I didn't even think any different. I still felt like Brandon, but still in a girl's body. The professor simply smirked at me when it was done, watching me freak out a little.

"Don't worry, ladies. It's temporary. And if little Katie here doesn't want to feel any of the effects, she shouldn't run into a man. Shouldn't be hard at this school for girls!"

The other girls laughed again. I relaxed a little. Maybe this was some kind of hazing. Maybe it was a prank they played on newcomers to the school.

"Too bad we have a very special guest today, come out here Gary!"

Oh shit. Oh shit. Oh shit. I closed my eyes and covered my face with my hands. I didn't know what was coming, but I didn't want to be here anymore.

I could hear gasps again, and fawning from the other girls. I heard the muffled sounds of footsteps approaching, which stopped in front of me. I sat at the front of the class. This was my own damn fault. I had this coming to me.

"Hello, Katie." I could hear the words lift like a soft and gentle breeze on the wind. They were spoken by a man. By a man to me. My brain lit up like it was waking from slumber. The spell... it must be...! I clenched my hands tighter to my face. Do not look at him, do not look!

A hand. A warm and comforting hand rested on my shoulder. I knew it was a man's hand. I could sense it. It was light, kind, but the small force of it startled me to release my blinds and look up into his face. His face. His!

The rest of the world fell away until it was just the two of us, looking at each other.

He was gorgeous.

I fell for him instantly.

"He-hello." I stammered like a fool. I wanted to impress him, to show him that I can be his. What does he like? Where is he from? Who can I be for him?

His next words change me. "You're beautiful, Katie."

He thinks I'm beautiful. Me. He likes the way that I am now, and right now I'm a woman. I can be his woman. I want to be his woman forever, if it would make him love me. He wants to call me Katie. Fine. I am Katie. It doesn't matter that I was someone else before, I'm his Katie now, if that would make him happy.

I see him looking at my body. He looks at my chest and smiles. He likes my breasts. He called me beautiful, so they must be beautiful too. I love my breasts, if he loves them.

Before I realize it, I'm standing before him. The rest of the class is there too, watching in silent awe. I ignore them, they're not really there. They don't matter to me right now.

He reaches around and hugs me, caressing my sides as he does it. He likes the shape of my body. I am a girl now, after all. He likes girls, then. He must. I can be a girl. I can be a *convincing* girl, if it would let me have him. I smile at him, and hold him. I look at his lips, wanting them.

Many girls like boys. I am a girl. So I might like boys. I can like boys, even if I never liked boys before. This is different, this is for him.

I feel warmth stirring in me. My insides burn with passion and anticipation. I've never felt like this before, but this must be what it is like to love a man. I want him. I want him inside me, loving me, loving the Katie that I have become.

I don't hear the murmurs of the class. Like, "what's wrong?" and "shouldn't it have worn off by now?" and cheers like "get it girl!" and "he's so hot!" I ignore them. This is my moment.

I get lost in time staring at him, and before I know it we are at his place. I'm naked, he's naked. This is natural. I'm a girl, and he's a hot, sexy, ferocious boy. I only want to make him happy, so I will stay his girl forever. I will be his Katie forever.

VII

Oh

TAGS: THE AUTHOR, EMILY, SEX, REALISTIC, WILLING

Dishes were done. Work was done for the night. She was in the bath-room, and I sat on the bed waiting for her. I was only wearing my boxers.

I pulled up my phone while I waited. A thought had occurred to me, and I wanted to jot down a few words.

"Okay, tell me, in great detail, what you like in a man."

Fuck. I'm not into men. I looked at my girlfriend Gwen, but she wasn't paying attention to me anymore. She had already sidled over to Dan and the two looked like they were flirting. Determined to make her jealous, I decided to go for it. What could go wrong? I wasn't a girl, I was only disguised as one. I shrugged my shoulders, and looked back at the guy.

"Well, I like big, strong, handsome guys. The type of guy that can pick me up, you know? Treat me nice, cook me dinner."

He looked almost bored. "Oh, is that all?"

Gwen was still not paying me any mind. I had to keep going. I had to double down. Somehow, I felt more confident this time.

"No, I like guys with cute, firm butts. A stubbly beard, tight abs." I found myself getting weirdly excited, but I needed my coup de grace to sell it.

"He should have a nice big dick, too."

"Hey sexy."

I'm snapped out of my world and look up from my phone to see Emily posing in the doorway, wearing her white lingerie from our wedding night. She's stunning.

"Oh wow, hey. You look nice." I said. She approached, calm and with confidence, and straddled me. I set my phone on the nightstand. She had shaved her legs, her skin felt smooth to the touch. She leaned in and kissed me. I wondered if she minded my beard at all. If she did, she never said anything.

I was getting hard, and I knew we couldn't do this with my boxers still on. I did a quick twist of my hips and guided her onto the bed, touching her with my mouth in as many places as I could to rediscover her. It was easy, I was so much bigger than her.

"You like that?"

"Well, I like big, strong, handsome guys. The type of guy that can pick me up, treat me nice, cook me dinner."

I slid my boxers off and pressed up against her. I wasn't fully hard yet, but I soon would be. I drank her softness, managing myself until I was stiff enough to—

"Oh!" She let out.

182

I got it. I understood sex. Ever since I lost my virginity in that tiny dorm room, I learned to chase the *Oh*. That sensation where a woman is so overcome with good feelings that her body is unable to contain the exhalation of a single sound as soft and vulnerable as *Oh*. A compulsion, a brief moment of such vulnerability shared between two people fucking that culminates in a revealed expression of bliss.

Sex was simple: you just needed to be vulnerable with each other.

I loved the laciness of her lingerie. The fabric was white and silky and smooth against our bodies as I worked my way in and out of her. I craved the way that clothing fit on women's bodies.

"When was the last time someone fingered you?"

No. Not now.

"Oh, my last boyfriend loved fingering me, so about a year ago. He was so good at hitting my sensitive spots and getting me to orgasm from that alone." I sighed, reliving the experience. I started to feel myself getting a little warm down there, and for whatever reason I was feeling much more comfortable in my tight jeans.

Fragments of my writing popped into my brain. I shoved them aside. This wasn't the time for that.

Instead I wondered what she was thinking about. She had a cute face and her hair was getting tangled in my mouth and in the sheets.

How much time had passed already?

She was no longer making sounds of pleasure. I can fix this. I lifted her legs to try and get a better position, maybe that would be better for her.

He thinks I'm beautiful. Me. He likes the way that I am now, and right now I'm a woman. I can be his woman. I want to be his woman forever, if it would make him love me. He wants to call me Katie. Fine. I am Katie. It doesn't matter that I was someone else before, I'm his Katie now, if that would make him happy.

My mind wandered to other stories I had written. Stories of twisted and torrid affairs I had read. Those always turned me on. Thinking of myself as a girl. Thinking of myself getting hypnotized or mind controlled and [[fucked.]]

Stop!
Stop thinking about that!
Let's focus. You're fucking your wife, remember? In, out, in, out. That's how it works, right?
I caressed her body and squeezed her tit. I've fucked her a million times. I know how to do this. I played with her ass and kissed her neck. I explored every inch of her body while fucking her.
Why am I not cumming? Why isn't she cumming?
I decided to try something different. I try a different rhythm. I go slower, more intentionally. Less chaotic. Am I bad at sex? How can I be bad at sex, I write about sex all the fucking time.

I feel warmth stirring in me. My insides burn with passion and anticipation. I've never felt like this before, but this must be what it is like to love a man. I want him. I want him inside me, loving me, loving the Katie that I have become.

Fuck it. I leaned into these idle thoughts. I could be Katie, or whatever. At least I knew I could cum this way. I closed my eyes and forgot about being the man. I tried to imagine myself as Katie, as the girl from the pizza place with the witchy tattoos. I imagined myself getting fucked instead. It's a weird kink, I told myself. But I'm allowed to have weird, secret kinks. I was sure everyone had them. Emily's probably thinking about someone else, anyway.

That's what I would do, [[if I was her.]]

"*Oh!*" She whimpered out, stammered a bit, and I felt her body tense up and shudder. The trick worked.

We laid there, her finger traced the bumps of my spine as our sweat mixed between our bodies. "Do you want to try to finish?" She asked.

"I don't know if I can tonight." I lied. "I don't think I have it in me."

"Oh. That's okay."

We clean up, grabbing an old t-shirt to use as a rag. She heads to the shower. I head to the other bathroom with my phone.

[[WISHES FROM A COIN]]

TAGS: TG, COIN, MAGICAL, UNWILLING, MIND CONTROL

"All right, I'm ready. Make a wish."

Jake and Dan were outcasts, and weren't able to get the dates they wanted to attend the end of the year ball at their school. However, Dan stumbled across an old magic shop that promised to solve their problems—it sold him a magical wishing coin.

"I wish for you to turn into a girl and that's it? Seems too easy." Dan shook his head, inspecting the curious gilded thing.

"Yeah. We will go as a couple, turn some heads, get you noticed as a guy capable of picking up a hot chick, and get out of there. No need for any funny stuff, no kissing, and I'll change back into a guy again. I trust you! In exchange, you'll do the same thing for me."

Shrugging, Jake held the coin firm in his palm and went for it. "I wish Dan was... a hot girl!"

Dan gasped as changes took hold of him. It was instantaneous, like the universe blinked and replaced the normally stocky dusty-haired Dan with a slim and blonde young woman. She stood there, mouth agape and looking over herself.

"This is incredible, it worked!" She said, twirling around. She winked at Jake. "How do I look?"

Jake had to take a moment to absorb the fact that the coin really was magical, and that his best friend stood before him as the hottest girl he'd ever seen. Jake swallowed his arousal.

"Let's get to the ball before I get too excited for this, Dan. Well, huh, I guess we should call you something else. How about Piper? I'm certain no one will be the wiser."

"Works for me!" Dan slipped on her dress they had gotten from a thrift store earlier, and they made their way to the party.

***

"Look who decided to show up! It's Jake! And who is *this* pretty young thing?"

That annoying voice came from the curled mouth of Adam Crabapple. What a dick, thought Dan. That guy was always roughing him up in the halls, backed up by his posse of obnoxious friends from the basketball team. Forcing a smile, Dan managed to squeak out a few words while he masked his disdain.

"I'm Piper, Jake's date for tonight. Nice to meet you."

Dan wrapped one arm around Jake's, and turned to leave with him. He stopped when Adam and his friends started laughing at them and calling him a "slut-for-hire." This wasn't going as well as they had planned. Jake reached into his pocket and pulled out the coin. He was ready to wish Adam would turn into a crab, but one of Adam's friends ripped it from his hand from behind. The whole thing happened so fast, Dan hardly had time to cry out.

"Hey, give that back!" Jake demanded.

"You wish! What were you going to do, throw this at us? Whole lotta good that would do you. I'm keeping the change." The boys laughed.

Dan steamed, visibly. "You stupid sacks of shit, give it back to us and leave us alone."

Dan tried to make himself look intimidating, but that proved to be difficult. He was far smaller than the guys now.

"Whoa, whoa, hey there." The guy flipped the coin in his hand. "I wish you would be more ladylike. We are in public, you know."

They all laughed again. Adam's friend tossed the coin over to Adam. A shiver trickled through Dan's spine as the wish settled in. Something clicked deep inside, throwing Dan off the tracks.

Piper shook her head, and smiled sweetly, "I'm sooo sorry guys, I don't know what came over me. May we please have the coin back? Jake and I would like to have a nice evening together."

Jake started to sweat. He was hoping maybe the wish didn't kick in so thoroughly for his friend, but he had to play along.

"Yeah, you heard…her. Can we please forget this whole thing and move along?" Adam sighed a bored sigh.

"Fine." He smiled at the hot girl on Jake's arm.

"Though I do wish you'd be *my* date for tonight. I think we'd have a lot of fun together."

That chill again. Piper felt like it would all be okay if she just gave in. Would it be so bad to be Adam's date for tonight? Probably not. And they *could* have a lot of fun.

"Sure! Why not?"

Piper let go of Jake's arm and sauntered over to Adam, to Jake's horror.

"...Piper? You okay?"

"Yeah! I'm fine. You go on ahead without me, we'll meet up later."

She winked at Jake, as she slipped her slender arm around Adam. Jake wasn't sure what the wink meant. Good wink? Bad wink? Either way, he still didn't have the coin.

"Damn, girl, you are pretty easily convinced!" Adam said as they walked arm in arm through the crowd. "You didn't want to be with a loser nobody like Jake anyway."

Piper knew the key to getting her manhood back was with that coin in her date's pocket. She had to figure out a way to get to it.

Maybe... "How about you and I find somewhere a little more private for a little while?" She cooed.

She figured if she had these feminine mannerisms, she should take advantage of them. Without flinching, Adam grabbed her arm and directed her to a back hallway. He looked around quickly to see if anyone had followed them—they hadn't—and looked hungrily at his date.

"I like that you aren't the hard-to-get type."

He leaned in and pressed his lips against hers. It was all Piper could do not to refuse it and vomit. She wasn't into guys.

But, this was a means to an end. She started working her hand into his trouser pockets, feeling around for the coin. All this while her tongue was wrapped around his.

Taking a moment to breathe, Adam said, "Someone's feeling lucky!"

He grabbed her slender hand in his pocket, and moved it so that she was touching his solid dick. She got desperate. After the quick touch of his hardened cock she revolted, went back to looking for the coin more forcefully until she had her hand on it, and yanked it from his pants.

"I wish...!" But she was too late. "Ah!"

Adam grabbed it from her hands again and with his other hand grabbed her and pulled her to the floor.

"What *is* this? Who are you anyway? You're so desperate for this coin, aren't you? What did you want to wish for, huh?"

Piper looked up at Adam, but said nothing.

"Here, I'll humor you."

Holding the coin like she was a second ago, "I wish you were hotter."

It happened in a flash. Piper's sexy girl-next-door look gave way to a summer-tanned beach babe body and a killer ass. It was what Adam preferred in girls, anyway.

"Holy shit."

"Happy now?" Piper crossed her arms and looked away from Adam. Her breasts were even bigger than before.

"Hell yeah I am. I have no idea what this is but you are *gorgeous* now, babe! This coin did that!?"

"Jake will be here any minute now to st—"

"Ah, well I wish you'd forget about Jake. I also wish Jake would forget about you. How's that?"

She blinked. "How's what?"

Adam smiled, "Exactly."

"Listen, Adam. I need that back so that I can get back to being myself again."

"What do you mean? You got me, you got a smoking hot body, girl. What more do you need?"

Piper was silent. She didn't want to admit she was actually a man. Adam thought she was a girl this whole time... giving that away might...

"I'll make things better for you, sweetheart. Trust me. I wish that you forgot about this silly coin and whatever it did to you, because you're perfect. I wish that you would accept the girl that you are right now, and that you would live happily as my girlfriend Piper from here on."

She shook her head again as her mind was jostled back into place. It was like waking up from a dream that felt like it had taken years to get through. When she finally cleared her head, she looked at her boyfriend and smiled.

"Sorry Adam, I'm not sure why we were fighting. I'd like it very much if we could please go back to making out?"

Adam pocketed something, and smiled. It warmed her heart to see him look at her like that. He held her in his arms, and they shared an intimate moment together.

Jake, meanwhile, didn't have a date to this stupid ball. He wasn't sure why he came here in the first place.

VIII

SALT AND SUN

TAGS: THE AUTHOR, FAMILY, DEATH, LIFE

Time passes differently at light speed. It's hard to realize how fast you're moving until you stop to look up.

How's work going? Not particularly well. People like me. I play my part pretty well. I'm not where I want to be. I'll quit someday.

How's your sister? She moved to Japan to teach English. I never see her. I get updates occasionally. I don't know the name of her boyfriend.

How's Emily? She's great. We're great.

How's your mom? She's been managing ever since the separation. She's mostly stopped asking for money to pay her rent now that she's got that new job.

How's your dad?

***

I occasionally got positive updates on Dad's life. He was traveling with this new woman. They went to the Grand Canyon; they went to Vegas. I had never been to either of those places. He told me that he was getting some degree in nursing at a community college. I didn't believe that for a second.

But he went ahead and did it. I had to do a double take when I saw a photo of him in a graduation cap and gown in his fifties.

He told me he had stopped smoking. He told me he was trying to finally quit drinking, too.

"Are you proud of me?" He asked me.

That was a simple question with a complicated answer. I had spent so much of my life resenting this man, the way he abused alcohol, his family, himself. The things he said, the things he did. And to change, he left Mom. Could he be forgiven? Could I be proud of him for turning his life around when it had impacted my life so firmly? Could such a person ever see a transformation like this in their life?

But my father was genuinely happy now. But his health had never been worse, his liver was bad. "Never get old, son." He liked to say whenever he felt bad.

I visited him for my birthday. He had gone to the fish market and splurged on the largest Alaskan King Crab legs he could find. We spread newspapers out on the table and his girlfriend brought out a big bowl of melted butter. We slathered the creatures in Old Bay and made a huge mess. It was incredible.

"I'm on the list for a liver transplant," he said. "It's going to be fine."

He and his partner came to our wedding in Seattle. He cried. He looked good in his suit. He was a proud man and my image of him had evolved. It was hard to visualize the pain from our past in quite the same way. He enjoyed his trip, took lots of photos, and went on a whale watching tour.

"Your dad's not doing well, you should come and see him." His partner told me.

Emily and I took a cross-country flight to New Jersey as soon as we heard he had been admitted to hospice care. The liver failure was advancing faster than we thought. No transplant in sight. It was too late for that now.

I hadn't seen Dad in a year. We entered the room he was staying in and saw him. He was awake, but his words were a bit slurred. He was tired, and his skin was yellow. His eyes lit up when he saw me.

He cried. "You came all that way to see me?"

The past was nothing. I was struck by disbelief and sadness, and I silently forgave him. I promised to return the next day. I came prepared to ask him lots of questions about his life. All he wanted to do was be present with me. I told him that I loved him. That I was proud of him.

"We had fun, didn't we?"

***

I clutched the tiny opaque black box in my hand. Dad's latest transformation. He wanted to be cremated. I received his ashes in the mailbox a week later.

The sound of the boat's engine droned on as we moved our way through Rosario Strait. It was a beautiful day, and the islands were a welcome sight. I wanted to feel small, and I always looked forward to getting out on the water with Emily's family. Getting to bring Dad along was a bonus. One last thing to do together.

"This looks like a good spot." Emily's father had brought us to a protected spit. We caught a buoy and set up chairs in the back of the boat. The air was breezy and warm and I took a long breath of it.

I opened the little black box and turned it over into the water.

I watched in silence as the dust of my father poured out and scattered wildly into the calm waters, until each speck was unrecognizable from the salt and sun reflections, bearing witness to his final return to nature. I wondered if it felt comforting.

***

"We're trying to have a baby." I told Dad on his deathbed. I was sad that he didn't get to see any grandchildren before he passed.

Emily and I had been trying for months, but we hadn't had any luck. She wondered if we had fertility problems. I wondered if it had anything to do with my now notorious inability to finish the job.

I remember the fights. I remember spending long nights passing time together watching TV and creating excuses for going to bed early. I was frequently too tired for sex. I wasn't up to it.

Then, by some miracle—

"Ahh!!"

A scream from the bathroom startled me up from the couch to run and help. I found her, hyperventilating and laughing, pointing at the little white plastic stick on the tiled floor.

Pregnancy test.

Positive!

My stomach curled.
The world shifted.
This was monumental.
This was it, right?
This was the moment?
This was the beginning of our new life.
This was what we had asked for.
This was everything.

My mind was clear, and I could taste the air of hope. We hugged and danced. It was happening! After so much difficulty and sadness and loss, we were finally getting our win. When the surge of adrenaline subsided and we drifted back to the ground, we took a moment to collect ourselves. This was bigger than either of us, and we had so much work to do.

I should stop.

This will be the reason I stop.

I won't write those stupid stories anymore. For our child, I'll stop.

I won't have to tell Emily that this was ever a problem if I just quit now.

In hindsight it feels like it only lasted a minute.

Another scream from the bathroom,

Sad, this time, because after

A few short, happy days,

Our baby was

gone

BODY

Kayla held fast the lines keeping her sails aloft. She had weathered these storms before. Over the past few years, she had written hundreds of stories and cast them out to the ghosts of the water. Masses of the hungry followed her wake, eager for her gifts. She remembered that she, too, had been hungry once.

Other ships came and went, but her stories grew in number. Kayla found herself a regular contributor to the transformation writing community. She had become respected, known. Other captains would hail her for guidance now. Her ship was magnificent. It reflected the sunlight off its salty coating.

The stories that fell to the water became a part of this ecosystem. It fed the ghosts who, like Kayla, wanted to feel something. She fed the ghosts and they lifted her up. They supported her growth. Reinforced her ship. Gave her strength and confidence. All so that she could write more stories for them.

You can't tell that the ocean is rising when you're in it, and Kayla realized she hadn't seen dry land in a long while.

The stories kept her busy, gave her purpose in this purposeless non-existence. She fed her ego by feeding the ghosts. They thanked

201

her, made her better, and promptly left. If she wanted to call them back, she'd have to write more stories.

But when did these stories end? And what about *her*? She wasn't telling a story about *her* life—she had none. Didn't the ghosts want to know who *she* was? What kind of person she was? Didn't they know that she was doing all of this for herself as much as she was doing it for them? She began to miss her Buddies, and she missed James. But there was no going back to that kind of life, was there? She'd have to lie again and break her own heart when forced to confront the truth.

What kind of person was she?

She was here forever.

The horizon line glimmered. In the distance, though foggy, something emerged that wasn't a ship or ghost. The shape bulged from the water and as her ship drew closer it grew larger. It had mass. Kayla stared with shocked awe as the land took form and broke her infinite lonely emptiness.

So: the ocean is the Internet, full of porn.

And the ghosts are the people who read or interact with this porn.

The ships are the vessels of the writers and creators, like Kayla, who put the porn into the world.

And the island represents the—

"Are we done with metaphors yet?" Kayla asked.

The island represents the firm ground on which Kayla can stand, if she wants to be a—

"Real person?" Kayla guessed.

Yeah, a real person. Maybe if she...

"—sets foot on the island, she could use it as a place to plant trees or seeds or whatever and feed the ghost fish for a thousand years and that would bring her closer to being able to *touch*, or whatever." Kayla said. "I get it."

You get it? Hold on, what's happening here?

"Well, here's the thing, the island didn't simply *appear*. You wrote it there for me to find. I don't need to set foot on this fake island to gain a foothold on my identity that you clearly want me to have. I know what it means. I'm tired of feeding the fish and not having anyone know who I am. I'm tired of not having a body like you to waste. You're somehow capable of writing these stories about sex and gender, but then you are *also* writing these stories about *me* and what I'm supposed to represent." Kayla said.

Well...

"You've written this whole thing about a repressed personality and took it on some romanticized 'growth' journey about *words* and *ships* and *buddies* and *oceans* and *bullshit*. You speak like there's a way out of this, but there's not. I'm just going to end up like one of your girls in your stories that's allowed to experience femininity but never allowed

to enjoy it. That's not romantic, that's torture. You've tortured me."
Kayla said.

I—

"Here's what happens next. I'm going to create a platform. For *myself*. I'll use my stories as a way to draw in more readers and build an audience. With a platform, I'll talk about *my* life. It might not be a life like yours, but maybe it'll be close enough to feel like one." Kayla said.

"I want to go on dates! I want to have good times, bad times. I can touch, I know I can. Me! Kayla! Not the empty mannequin girls in your fucking stories. People out there already know my name, but now they can get to know me, too. I won't have to explain myself to anyone. I'm going to have that physical euphoria. I'm going to feel it. We'll both feel it." Kayla said.

"I can be really convincing—you know that better than anyone. If writing these stories gave me purpose, maybe this will give me life. So, thank you for cracking the window to let a little light in. I've got it from here." Kayla said.

LIFE IN TWO

TAGS: THE AUTHOR, EMILY, UNWILLING, KAYLA, WILLING

I woke as a labored titan to the sound of Emily's morning shower. She always woke up before I did. She was always better at that than me. She was more motivated than I was and liked to get things done in the morning.

I groaned as I sat my mass up in bed. I ran a hand through the greasy prickle of my short hair and scritched the itchiness of my scraggly beard. I hated this thing. I only kept it because Emily told me she liked it.

I reached for my phone and opened Kayla's Tumblr account. She had already received a bunch of reactions to the latest story she'd posted last night.

> **Fadingroyalmuse21** Wow girl, that was SUPER FUCKING hot. :P
>
> **Lovebigdaddy78** hey babe, what u doin
>
> **Stranger18783692** Good morning Kayla :)

I didn't care about these perverts. These faceless, horny creeps that craved attention from an attractive girl like Kayla. They fought amongst each other in the comment section for scraps of validation, screaming out in small font voices to the dark so that something might register their pain as valuable. Still, my fingers moved independent of my conscious brain as I typed sweet responses to each of them.

Kayla Thanks darling! Glad you liked it! <3

Kayla Heyyyyy not much just waking up, wbu

Kayla Morning!!!

Kayla was more awake than I was.

lovebigdaddy78 what you wearing today babe

Kayla think i'll break out my favorite sundress :) it's gorgeous outside

I threw on the black shirt with the screen printed logo I got for free from work, and a pair of large time-worn jeans that wouldn't stay up without a belt. They were loose at the ends and the fabric had frayed at the heel. My old sneakers were dirt-stained, flat at the sole. It looked like I'd need to wear a company-issued hoodie too: a big storm was coming.

Every day I would drop Emily off on our way to work as part of the morning commute. When she got out of the car, I checked my messages again before driving the rest of the way.

Godofthefutas What are you up to today, Kayla?

Kayla I'm taking the day off to hang out with my boyfriend at the park. Then he's cooking me dinner at his place! :)

Godofthefutas Oooh lucky guy.

Kayla Lucky him? Lucky me! He's gorgeous.

Kayla had a life of her own. Whenever the phone was on, she was on. She chatted with her friends and reblogged content and posted comments and checked in on people she hadn't talked to in a while. She had an ironclad backstory. A boyfriend with a name. Ex-boyfriends who she could go on for hours about how they did her wrong. She had periods, imperfections, bad days, good days, and stories to tell. She was indistinguishable from a real person. She was untouchably cool. The kind of girl I'd like to get to know someday. It's no wonder people liked her.

I clocked in and sat at my desk and worked. Phone calls and meetings all day. When I was ready for a bathroom break, I sat in the stall with my phone out.

Pancaliguy8 When's your next story coming out?

Kayla Soon! I've got a few ideas brewing.

Pancaliguy8 Nice. Your last story was so hot, you're such a great writer.

Kayla Awwww thanks hun.

Pancaliguy8 Why do you write this stuff anyway? Aren't you a girl?

Kayla I dunno. I guess it turns me on. I like these stories and it's a good excuse to stretch my creative muscles. Besides, I get to talk to people like you. :)

Her execution was unmatched; she was perfect. I admired her for working as hard as she did. The door to the restroom squeaked open and I'm reminded that I've been in here for at least fifteen minutes. I washed up and got back to work.

My boss said something I would have disagreed with, but I'm not there. Kayla is thinking about how she might frame the story she'll be working on for tonight. First person perspective or third person omniscient? First person is sexier, somehow; third person perspective always feels so removed from the emotion.

And so, the sad 30-year-old man with an online persona he has let take over his life drives home to his condo. He kisses his wife, and she prepares a simple dinner. While she cooks, he logs on to the app on his phone in secret and waxes poetic to an admiring fan.

Kayla My boyfriend is making me salmon. Yum!

When someone like this lives inside your head, you're never alone. Free time is the crack by which this inner person squeezes through, so all available time goes to them. I'd wake up in the morning and check my phone, brush my teeth, check my phone, eat some food, check my phone, stop at stop lights, check my phone, do some work, check my phone. I'd check my phone before and after sex, before and after dinner, before bed, in bed, after bed. When I wasn't completely occupied with something or someone in front of me, that time went to Kayla.

I hated Kayla for doing this to me, for making me feel so powerless to stop it. I sat for dinner, my phone resting in my pants pocket. I wondered if Kayla had received any messages lately. Of course, I knew that she had. She was good at not only talking with people, but also with creating content that inspired people to talk to her. Kayla was a terrible combination of lonely and charismatic, which made it that much harder for me to retain control of my own free time.

I looked up from the food Emily had prepared and saw that she was sitting in silence, staring at me. Trying to understand why I'd zoned out for so long. I couldn't even tell how much time had passed while I was worrying about Kayla.

"You got something on your mind?" She asked, concerned with a hint of annoyance.

"No." I said. "Just enjoying the meal."

Sissyhypnobear liked your post

I found myself logging onto Tumblr a lot more often when I was sad or angry or frustrated. Mostly I felt numb to a lot of things. What else could I do to pass the time but be a person with an entirely different story than mine? A person who told stories that other people liked. A good friend, someone that people found worthy of admiring. Someone who was present, attentive, loving, fun.

Papalikesthat33 liked your post

It felt like I was cheating on Emily with this person I invented. I flirted with her. I had sex with her. I spent my waking hours day-dreaming about her. Why was I like this? Had I simply written Kayla into the threads of my life so much that I'd forgotten myself?

I needed Kayla to be completely fleshed out. If she couldn't be a complete person, neither could I.

Thegoose reblogged your post

But Kayla held the reins now. Not a day went by when she wasn't posting something tantalizing to her feed. She grew more confident as her online empire expanded.

I could hear the *click-clack* of her sharp heels on the hardwood floor in my head; a young woman with styled wavy ginger hair and a custom tailored business suit was on an important phone call.

"We need two 2,000 word stories by Tuesday, or we aren't going to meet our goal." She said, "I don't care *how* you transform them this time. Do I need to do it myself?" She looked annoyed, but she kept the same walking pace. Never too flustered to stop. Never ever stopping.

Hornygurrrl liked your post

"Sorry, I'm getting another call. Hello? Oh yes, you're looking for another post?" She pulled out a notepad from her purse, hooking her cellphone in a pink jewel-studded case between her ear and shoulder. "Updates on my boyfriend, details about my sex life, got it. Anything else? I can get right on that."

Onehundredmonkeys reblogged your post

Call after call. Each story, each post, carefully planned and executed. The demands poured in, and each time, she'd come to me.

Kayla halted her walking, and the scene froze around her. She turned to face me. "That's right, I go to you. Where else am I supposed to get the time for all of this?"

jennyCD_27 started following you

My brain is so full of these thoughts, Kayla. It's too much. I want to stop.

"Uh, hello? We have all these people out here now that are counting on us for this content. This isn't *just* for me, you know. Or for you, I guess, for that matter." She gestured broadly to the thousands of followers we'd accumulated so far. She smelled like vanilla. I wasn't sure how she managed to do that.

chumbawumba9000 started following you

Ugh. Stop. Please stop. This is all too overwhelming, Kayla. Where does it end? How long do we have to keep doing this?

shemale456 liked your post

"I don't see a way for us to stop. Unless you want to kill me!" She laughed. "I'm certainly not going quietly on my own, that's for sure. I've worked too hard for this. Now look, let's make a post about my latest date and forget about this whole thing."

You're such a slut.

7Freddddd liked your post

She stiffened, stopping in place and turning to face me. She has to. A cold bath of fear washed through her. "Excuse me?"

I made you, right? I can make you act however I want you to act. I want you *gone* but I can't seem to have that, so maybe if I make you a perfect little whore you'll grow tired and go away. Is that what it takes? This is my book, Kayla! You keep getting in the way.

"Are you joking? How will that solve anything? You can't write me out of the book. You can't write any of this away!"

Transhole69 liked your post

You're not a real person.

You're fiction! I made you up. You don't have control over me.

You're just a horny slut. You have no place in my life.

You've ruined it, you've ruined it!

"I..." Kayla started, but I make her stop talking.

Her mind was all "like, super foggy" now.

You're a useless, brainless whore now. This is what you deserve.

She giggles, she's a childish fool. An airheaded bubble in the wind.

Why can't you shut the fuck up and leave me alone?

I used to be happy. I was supposed to be happy!

Kayla is a dumb, stupid, bitch. Fuck you.

I'm going to stop writing about you. I uninstall Tumblr.

I delete the draft of the most recent story from the notepad file.

I close all the tabs of naked, faceless Kaylas in Private mode.

I delete all the hidden photos in my photo apps.

I delete everything.

She goes away forever. She's nothing. She never existed.

Kayla dies. Her non-blood pools around her non-lifeless non-body.

She's fucking dead.

This page is blank.

This one too.

I don't want to do this anymore.

You see that there's more of this book left to read, don't you?

Obviously this isn't the end of the story.

I'm not so foolish to think that I can keep you from turning these pages. But every word you've read has forced this awful story to progress. **You** *did this to me. All of you so-called "supportive" readers out there encouraged me to keep writing those terrible stories.*

I need time to think. I need to escape the disquiet.

Where's the most comfortable page in this book, you think? Where can one stay forever, free from the trauma that led them there, free from the future repercussions of their actions? An ever-cycling and blissful present. If you can find it, do me a favor and read that one over and over again.

I don't want your lessons! I don't want to face what comes next. I don't want you to keep reading. You don't have to. She's finally dead.

And what's your deal?
Are you feeling compassionate by reading these words?
Do you think I'm proud to write them for you?
I hate this.
Put the book down, forget about all of this.
Let me live here, on this page, forever.

THE HOSTAGE

[[THE HOSTAGE]]

Tags: TG, Realistic, Magical, Unwilling, Murder, Kidnapped, Rape, Kayla

My legs were giving out beneath me. I couldn't keep running.

Shouts echoed through the halls. "I'll find you, Brian! You can't hide forever!"

Gasping, I found myself at the end of this laboratory. No way out. Shit. I slammed into one of the rooms and looked for a quick escape option. The windows were too thick, and my only other opportunity was back where I came from. Through Jack. The man who was going to kill me.

Desperate, I scanned the room for a weapon. What caught my eye was a large box that resembled a casket, I pried it open with my bare hands, shocked to find what looked like a life-sized model. It was a woman, but she was split in half?

Hearing his footsteps closing in on me through the halls I made a desperation move and slipped in between the two pieces of the female mannequin and closed the casket. The box smelled like rubber.

The door opened and shut. Fuck. Fuck. Fuck. Why did I pick this box to hide in? This is a shitty place to hide. I'm going to fucking die in this casket!

"Alright Brian. I know you're in here somewhere…" he muttered. "Come out, and maybe I'll strike you a deal."

I squirmed, and heard the sound of a switch being thrown. The box I was in started humming, and I began to feel like my skin was… crawling.

"What the…" I heard Jack exclaim from outside the chamber. "Brian! I know you're fuckin' in there!"

I wanted to sink into the floor, this was where I would die. I could feel him trying to pry open the box, but it wouldn't give. All the while, I felt like my legs were melting, and the sensation creeped up my whole body like an ooze.

Jack pounded on the box repeatedly, and I was powerless to escape. My groin burned, like my dick was caught in a trap. I felt it grow harder despite the circumstances, and I let out a small yell as I felt a strong push against it. I felt like it was being crammed inside me.

The rubber of the mannequin squeezed me, was I being crushed? I couldn't move a muscle as my bones groaned and cracked. I was dying. My chest heaved against my labored breath, the ooze seeping into my skin. I felt hotter. The ooze made its way to my face, and the sounds of Jack's cries grew muffled. I was drowning in plastic, I couldn't breathe.

The lightless interior of the box grew darker as my eyes were covered. The top of my head crawled as well, but I knew there was nothing I could do. Resigned to my fate, I waited to die.

"Euuuuuhhhhhhhhh!" I gasped as my throat was somehow cleared of the material. My eyes were thrown open, and the buzzing box stopped. I could hear Jack still pounding on it, and a second later he grabbed the side of the casket and lifted it open.

"What..." Jack and I finally met face to face. But he was looking at me oddly, staring at my entire body in disbelief. "You're a... you're not Brian."

Confused and more than a little terrified, I looked down at my own body. I was naked, and had two fleshy mounds on my chest. Tits, I thought to myself. My hand raced to my groin where I was met with a smooth landing and a wet softness. It was warm to the touch, and startled me. I was...

"A girl!?" I shrieked, surprised yet again that my voice had changed. My long hair swayed in front of me as I struggled with this reality.

Jack stared at me as I continued to freak out, at the machine I was still lying in. "So... you are Brian after all." His expression turned. "Maybe this will be more fun than killing you. After all, if I can't turn in the man who stole 5 million dollars from my boss, perhaps I can live with a substitute as hot as you are."

I shook my head, taken aback by his stare as his eyes bore into me, "...what?"

He drew a small knife from a holster on his waist, leaned in over me and pressed it up against my neck. I could feel its sharpness, and I held my breath so as to not have my flesh rub against it.

"You're coming with me, Brian. You're going to tell me where you hid the cash, and I'm going to let you live."

I swallowed, the harsh blade gripping into my neck. I whined a little, expressing understanding into Jack's eyes. It looked like he got my message, as his smile crept back to his lips.

Just as quickly as he pulled it out, he slipped the blade away. "Good girl."

I winced as he grabbed some rope from a corner of the room. I couldn't escape! He commanded me to stay still while he tied the rough material around my skinny wrists, binding my legs. He took his time fashioning a restraint around my chest, grazing my breasts with his fingers.

He tore some duct tape and placed it over my mouth. "In case you get any ideas." He said. Then he lifted me, completely bound, and carried me out of the lab to his van outside.

***

The van doors swung open and my dilated pupils caught too much sunlight. Not that being blinded mattered. I was still semi-hog-tied, captured by a man that wanted to kill me, and, oh, I had tits now. I hardly had time to come to terms with my transformation at the lab. To make things worse, I was still naked. Every bump in the road bounced my new breasts, and I felt the awkward sensation of an actual pussy between my legs as I struggled against my bonds. I tried screaming, only to hear my new high-pitched shrill muffled behind the duct tape

225

across my lips. My hair was longer, and I was hardly the same shape that I was before.

"Alright, come on." Jack grunted as he lifted my nubile body from the van, my hairless legs dangling. He was taking me into his house! The door was kicked closed behind him, and he dropped me onto his leather sofa. I could only watch him as he dropped off his keys and checked his phone for messages.

"Okay, so somehow you got yourself turned into a broad." He finally said, staring at his prize from across the living room. "I'm not sure how you managed to do that, but that doesn't matter now."

He took a few steps towards me and knelt beside the couch, gripping my hair and pulling my head to look right at him. My breathing was labored, it was not easy breathing through my nose for this long.

"You're going to tell me where you hid the money."

The money. The 5 million dollars in the abandoned suitcase I found in the nightclub. The suitcase that I buried in the graveyard 10 miles out of town. The gravestone of some guy named Barnabus J. Green. Green, for money. I shook my head. I wasn't entirely sure I was being sane, myself. But what were the chances he'd let me live even if I *did* tell him? His smile turned to a frown.

"You fucker. You've gone through all this, turned yourself into a fuckin' dame, and you're not gonna fucking tell me where the money is?" He thought for a moment, running his hand along my back. "Maybe if I fuck you you'll think differently, huh?"

I closed my eyes. His hand caressed my side, groping its way to my bottom which was still in the air, my legs still tied. His fingers curved and snuck in between the cleft leading to my pussy. His hands trembled in both anger and anticipation, and my body tensed up. "You have such a nice ass now, Brian. Hard to imagine you were ever a man, huh?"

My body was shocked like it was hit by lightning as he jabbed a finger into my pussy. I had never felt so penetrated before, and Jack did it with such vile intentions, he laughed a little as I squirmed awkwardly on the couch. "What, never been fingered before, huh? Tell me where you hid it, I'll make it stop!"

I clenched my teeth and squeezed my eyes together as I felt him wiggle his fingers around my pussy. He dipped in and out, exploring the folds. I could feel him inside me, and as he finger-fucked me I began to understand my own inner workings better. My body grew hotter, and I could feel blood rushing from all corners of my female body rushing to receive the sexual signals. Whether I liked it or not (and I hated it), my pussy grew wetter and wetter. I screamed again into the duct tape. I heard the sound of his pants unzipping shortly after I no longer felt his finger violating me.

No, no! I screamed and cried again into the tape. He climbed behind me and I felt concentrated flesh against my ass, followed swiftly by my entire vagina filled wall-to-wall with his dick. I couldn't look at him as my face was pushed into the sofa. "It's a good thing you're hot, Brian. Or should I rename you? Yeah, you'll be my little bitch. If you don't want to give me the cash, I'll have to chain you up downstairs. Make you my whore, would you like that, huh!?" My body tensed further as his rod rammed into me. He gripped my ass roughly, but I started to lose all sense of time. Over and over again I could feel dick deep inside my vagina. I stopped screaming at some point.

The front door opened sometime as he was still fucking me. Sounds were muffled "Jack, what the fuck is this!?"

Exhausted, I turned my head enough and caught a glimpse of a large man looking at the scene. Jack stopped thrusting and pulled his dick out of me with a wet 'pop.'

"Oh, Harry, I was just..."

"You were just what, Jack? You kidnap this girl or something, is she some whore? You're supposed to be getting my fucking money!!" I could feel cum dripping out from me.

"No, it's not what it looks like, I was just..." The man grabbed Jack by the neck and tossed him to the ground. "You were supposed to be working, not fucking around. I'll have to find someone else to do it now."

Before Jack could launch into pleas, the man pulled out a small gun and shot him square in the heart.

My eyes were wide with terror. I was still tied up and sore, and I saw the one man who knew who I was get killed. Harry stood and walked over to me, and started to untie my bonds.

"Sorry you had to see that. Had to be done, no one lies behind my back and gets away with it. At least he can't rape you anymore." I steadily sat up and faced him, he was massive. He was the guy I stole the cash from. I brushed my hair from my face. "Alright, girl, what's your name?"

***

"Well? What's your name?" Harry towered over my petite female frame. I still hadn't recovered from him killing Jack in front of me, let alone that I had been fucked—as a woman—by a man. But, Harry doesn't know who I am. This could be an opportunity for me to escape.

"...Kayla." I lied.

"Are you some whore Jack picked up? What's the story there?"

I thought fast. This guy was clearly powerful, maybe I should try and earn brownie points with him.

"He kidnapped me. He kept talking about how he found 5 million dollars after killing a man named Brian, and was going to take me for his... wife. I think he meant to betray you..." I shifted in my seat, trying to cover my still naked body.

"Did he ever tell you where the money went?" Harry leaned in, trying to read me. After he sensed even a small hesitation from me, he added "And don't worry, if you tell me, I won't harm you. I don't beat chicks like that fucker. Maybe I'll even find it in my heart to reward you."

My eyes lingered on the dead body once more. This was it. I mean, I had nowhere to go. I was a girl now, for fucks sake. "Yeah." I nodded. "I know where he hid it. He... wouldn't shut up about it." I added. I winced a bit as Harry stood, content.

"Where are your clothes?"

"He... he destroyed them."

229

"Well, let's get you something to wear." I rummaged through Jack's clothing drawer and pulled out some things. When I was still a guy I would have fit these just fine, but as a girl they hung on me like oversized bed sheets. The sweatshirt I pulled over my head hid my breasts pretty well, but it was a weird sensation having my nipples rub against the fabric. I found some camo pajama bottoms, pulled them up my legs and tied the drawstring as tight as it would go. I caught a glimpse of myself in the mirror. I looked like somebody's hot girlfriend on laundry day. Fuckin' weird.

Harry laughed. "You're okay wearing that?"

I didn't respond, as it wasn't clear if I should be making jokes with this guy or laying low around him.

"Don't worry, Kayla. I won't bite." He winked, and patted my ass as we walked out of the crime scene and jumped in his Ferrari.

"Holy god damn you weren't kidding, Kayla." Harry exclaimed as he dug up the grave lot I directed him to. He flung the dirt to my feet and revealed the briefcase. I kicked myself mentally, not believing that I found myself in this mess and now I don't even have the money to fall back on. Harry would've killed me for sure if I didn't give him this lead.

He clicked the case open, revealing the bricks of cash. Harry closed it again, beaming. "Alright, you and I have got to celebrate. I'll even spend some of this money on you, I hate when the figure of a beautiful woman is wasted under men's clothing."

I was hardly in the mood to celebrate, but what choice did I have? He took me next to his mansion. It was private—very private. We must have driven through the woods for 20 minutes before arriving at a gleaming palace of a home. Several people were hurrying about with various chores.

"Harry," I started, "how do you make your money?"

"I work in... sales." His face had the look of a man who didn't want me to ask him any more questions. So I didn't. He led me through the house. "That can be your room. It was my ex-wife's private space, I think you'll find anything you need here. Be ready in an hour."

It was large, filled with wardrobes and cabinets with a surprising ton of women's clothing stores within. A massive makeup station, fully stocked, rested in the corner; and a bed with overly pink sheets sat in the other corner. "What happened to you—" I started, but Harry had already left.

It was the first time I could be by myself and reflect on my position. I stripped naked again and examined my body. Reaching around and feeling every inch of myself I couldn't find a seam, or any trace of that weird plastic material that created this... transformation. It seemed thorough, even so far as to give me what I assumed was a perfect vagina. No time to lose. I was supposed to be celebrating with who is probably a huge drug lord that murders without care, dressed in his ex-wife's clothing, on the same day I was turned into a girl, kidnapped, and raped.

I slipped on a pair of the silkiest panties I've seen in my entire life and checked myself out in the mirror. I couldn't imagine this getting any worse, so it was time to play along. It was unclear where I was going with this, but if I was going to have any chance of survival, I needed to get on Harry's good side. An hour later I emerged from the room, dressed to the nines. It took forever to figure out how this dress worked, and the makeup job wasn't perfect, but it felt convincing.

Judging by the look I got from Harry, I was fuckin' hot. "Are you ready to celebrate?"

***

"I said... What'll you have, Miss?" The waiter asked me, somewhat impatiently. Being called Miss didn't quite register with me.

"Um," I glanced back at the menu, shivering a little. My knees were still somewhat chilly from being so exposed in this short dress. "I'll have the halibut, I guess."

The waiter took our menus, and I was forced yet again to endure staring at Harry. He didn't seem to mind looking at me, though, and his eyes wandered more than mine.

"So, Kayla, tell me about yourself. This is a safe place." He clasped his hands and rested his chin on them, eager.

I sat back, a bit tense. "I'm not sure I'm feeling very talkative after..." my thoughts trailed to the image of Jack, shot dead on the floor.

"What, that?" He chuckled. "Trust me, Kayla, no one treats a woman like that in my employ, and no one betrays my trust either." His eyes filled with a brief spark and his tone got darker. "No one."

I coughed. "If you'll excuse me, uh, I need to use the, um, ladies' room." I stood and he waved at me to go ahead. Stepping away, I wiped some sweat from my brow and ducked into the bathroom, where I stood once again face-to-face with my girlish reflection.

"Tough night?" An older woman asked nonchalantly, while she touched up her lipstick a few sinks over.

I shook off the stress as best I could. "You could say that, I guess."

"I saw you and your husband walk in. You two make quite an attractive couple!" She smiled at me, her makeup flawless.

"Oh, he—he's not my—" I gagged on the words. The woman laughed.

"Sorry! I merely assumed by the way he looks at you. You must have him eating out of your hand. You know, you could probably get him to do whatever you wanted."

With that, she left me alone. Whatever I want? I cupped my breasts through the dress, feeling their fullness and their weight in my hand. They were remarkably sensitive to the touch. I thought about all that money I had recovered for him, about how he stowed it away in his safe, about how maybe I could persuade him to let me have some of it. If I had even a fraction of that cash, I might be able to find a way back to manhood.

"Feeling better?" Harry asked as I sat.

I was determined. I was going to do this. Crossing my legs and smiling as wide as I could, I nodded. "Much better. And I wanted to thank you for taking me out tonight, this place is so charming."

We talked and ate, with me doing my best flirtatious girl impersonation. I made up stories about my childhood as a girl, talked about ex boyfriends I never had, and described my perfect man while rubbing my bare calf against his leg under the table. Harry looked increasingly interested as the night dragged on. When we got back to his place, I felt jittery. I knew what to expect—I had already been fucked as a girl once—but I hoped maybe it would be easier this time.

Harry wasted no time when we got inside, pulling me close to him and kissing me while squeezing my ass. It felt different than it had with Jack.

Perhaps it was the wine we had, but I felt myself drawn more fully into my little impression. I was wearing exceedingly girly clothes, making minx-like moans as we made out, and wobbling drunkenly in my stiletto heels. His hands roamed up the back of my dress, his fingers neatly tucked into my panties. I had never willingly kissed a man before, I reminded myself in our tense fervor, but my body craved the attention. Allowing myself to drift into the role of sexy babe about to get fucked by a big, strong man turned me on.

I made up my mind, or maybe it was made for me. Starting tonight, I would be Harry's girl. And if I played the part well enough, I could maybe get all that money back... The rest of our encounter swept me over like a dream. He tore my dress over my head and lifted me onto the kitchen counter. He stripped himself while he kissed me, massaged my thighs and prepared me for what was to come.

I was on fire, and I allowed myself into erotic bliss as my man fucked me.

X

THERAPY

Quiet.

With the exception of the ringing in my ears.

The movement of my body breathing, my heart doing its thing to keep blood circulating through my veins.

The sensation you get when you have the space to concentrate on the dull rubbing feeling of muscles working to shift your eyeballs around. Hands never sitting still.

The constant awareness of it all.

The stray thought that I missed my dad.

I opened my eyes and saw the large conference hall full of people sitting silent on expensive yoga mats and towels. The instructor stopped talking like an hour ago. "Mindfulness meditation retreat." I didn't want to be here. Who would want to be here?

Emily wanted to be here. I couldn't imagine why.

She asked me, "Why don't you want to go?"

"I just don't, okay?" I answered.

237

I know what happens when people go to therapy. They have to confront things. They have to feel things. Tear open the wound that is already bursting at the seams in a hidden place. The place you diligently cemented over years ago.

But I went—that's what good husbands do. I showed up with the yoga mat she bought for me that I never used. I laid on my back and stared at the ceiling, not talking. Sitting with my thoughts. This is dumb. This will never work. This will never heal me. All it will do is waste my Saturday.

We weren't allowed to talk during the six-hour retreat, but somehow Emily and I managed to fight anyway, exchanging cutting grimaces as two glaciers slicing through each other. I made her feel like she was forced to drag her sick, miserable, whining old dog to something she was genuinely looking forward to. Of *course* I felt bad about it, but there was no way I could feign enthusiasm about it now. I watched as a man paused to stare curiously at a small tree and pretended to be gratefully soaking in the sunshine. I wondered if he hated it too.

The dirt at my feet seems strong, but the air feels all wrong.

I feel vulnerable, like I could be engulfed at any moment.

***

Later, Emily and I sat in a waiting room together. There's plants on a windowsill that I don't know the names of. I stared at my hands, feeling like a kid who had done something wrong twiddling their thumbs patiently for their parents to come and get them.

"You can both come in," the woman said.

"I don't do therapy," I said. I didn't know what to say.

"Well, you can start with why you're here."

So Emily filled her in on the story. She has a sad husband who says mean things sometimes. She says mean things too. We have a hard time communicating. Sex is bad. His dad is dead. We lost a baby in a miscarriage. He hates his job and is incapable of leaving to get a new one. We're struggling.

[[I can't stop writing TG fiction, and won't tell anyone.]]

I make a mental note. I decided that now's not the time.

She turned to me to ask about my dad, my parents. I told her. She told me I am likely depressed and suffering from childhood PTSD. I should probably see a separate therapist to focus on that. I hate that idea, but agree that it's probably a good plan. I don't want to seem unreasonable.

"Would you feel more comfortable with a man or a woman therapist?"

[[Woman, of course. Talking openly with men feels weird.]]

I chose to talk with the man.

Fast forward: I'm sitting in an office with a bored-looking man who asks me to tell him about myself. He's chubby and has a beard. His haircut looks like mine, short and brown with a light powdering of gray. He looks a little like me. He sits in his big lounge-y chair to fit his big lounge-y body. I want to run but instead I tell him that I'm struggling at work. We talk about work things. I never mention my writing.

I don't go back.

We keep going to couple's counseling, though, and try to learn the words to be a productive married couple again. She wants me to be more romantically proactive. I learn to say when I feel things in response to things that she says. We go back and forth, back and forth, back and forth and continue our married existence. We go to work, come home and talk about our days, cook dinner, watch TV, see friends, make love, and age.

This is life, right? Life is the thing that happens to us. We're the couple that found each other and fell in love. The couple that ran away to Washington to build a home and become human. We got married, bought a condo, made careers, had setbacks and victories, and spent the long quiet next to each other to persist against the winds of time. The couple that would pause to pursue small pleasantries like staring at trees in awe and not think about how that might be a waste of our precious minutes.

The couple that would go to a six-hour retreat together specifically to say nothing to each other.

Weeks pass, and Emily's feeling unwell. Queasy.
She's felt this way before.
A white stick with a little blue cross rests on the bathroom tile.
The world has shifted once again.

[[REMOTELY INTERESTING]]

Tags: TG, Magic, Remote, Unwilling, Unaware, Tricked, Kayla

Oh no. No no no. Not like this.

"Um, I'm sorry. Who are you again? What are you doing in my room?"

"I told you. I'm your best friend, Greg. You were the one who turned me into this, and you somehow made a mistake with the remote and wiped your own fucking memory you moron!"

"Greg is no name for a girl as pretty as you are..." Scott mumbled, still reeling from the shockwave that scrambled his brain. I didn't know how to use the remote, and I was pretty sure Scott didn't know anymore either. I glanced at my new tits, the gentle curvature of my now much younger female body, and sighed.

If I tried to use the remote, I might wipe my own memory, and where would that leave me? "Fuck, man. I can't believe you did this to me, and now I'm not sure I can turn back into a guy again."

Scott held his head like it was throbbing. "A guy? Why would you ever want to turn into a guy? You're beautiful..." He stumbled over to me, drunkenly, and hugged me for support.

Disgusted, I brought my hands up and pushed him off me. "No! We need to get your memory back so you can fix me!" I squirmed, this girl's body felt so alien to me. Not having a dick was like a missing puzzle piece, I felt so empty.

I stared at Scott. He was useless, largely drooling on the floor at this point. Fuck me. I picked up the remote and tried to make sense of it. Maybe there was an undo button? Nothing was even labeled on this damn thing... I could turn myself into a chinchilla for all I knew. Setting the remote on the table, I evaluated my options. Change my name? Move to another city? Become a... lesbian?

I looked at Scott and realized my other option: Stay close to him, and help him remember how the remote works. He'll *have* to change me back into a man.

I spent the next few nights at Scott's place. He was almost entirely worthless alone, and I had to remind him that it was his house, who the people in his photo albums were, and tried to bring him around to relearning his remote device. For whatever reason I was incapable of explaining to him that I'm not actually a girl, and that it was his fault.

"Have you figured it out yet?" I asked, dropping the groceries on the kitchen counter. Running errands as a girl was certainly interesting, and no matter what I wore I couldn't avoid the gazes of men.

"I think so!" He exclaimed happily. "Though I'm still not sure why you'd ever want to be a man..." He configured some buttons on the remote and pointed it at me. I crossed my fingers and closed my eyes, and waited.

"...well?" I asked. I didn't feel anything. I opened one eye and saw Scott examining the remote again.

"Guess it didn't work." He mused. "I'll try some other stuff later."

"Fine." I crossed my arms. "I have some things I need to do today anyway. This place is a mess, you know that, right?" I huffed.

After spending the day cleaning the apartment, I couldn't help but think there was something off. Maybe I was growing more confident in this new skin. The next day was similar. I went out to do some clothes shopping. I needed some bras, I couldn't live without them forever. My former boxers hardly fit either, so I picked up some panties too. When I got back Scott was still tinkering with the remote.

"You ready?" He asked. I nodded. Crossed my fingers, closed my eyes. Again, nothing happened.

"Damn it, Scott." I pouted, my hand on my hip. "Please keep working on it, I'd really like to be a boy again..."

"Hmmm... yeah, not quite there yet. I have some other ideas, though."

That night I figured I should get out of the house. Maybe go to a bar or something. Not like I wasn't used to people seeing me as a girl at this point. For some reason, I felt comfortable enough putting on a dress, and even applied a little makeup

I had picked up from the pharmacy. Nothing too over the top, subtle blue eyeshadow to make my eyes pop a bit. I checked my reflection in the mirror. Yeah, I was pretty hot.

As I was about to leave, Scott stopped me in the doorway. "Hey, um, Greg. Looking good. I have something else to try!"

"I don't know, Scott. You keep trying but I'm starting to think it's not helping. Maybe you should take a break..."

"Nonsense! I want to help you out. Besides, don't you want to be yourself again?"

Before I could object further, he pointed the remote at me and clicked the button. Still, nothing happened. Frustrated, I pulled a hair behind my ear and sighed. "Ugh, come on Scotty. You need to fix that dumb thing. Like, I am so tired of it not working! Also, please don't call me Greg, okay? It's such a boy's name. Call me, like, Kayla or something."

Scott wrinkled his face, "Oh. Okay, uh, Kayla. I'll keep working on it. Have fun tonight!" Scoffing, I left for the club.

It was so freeing to let myself loose for a change! The music was pumping, the drinks were awesome, and I couldn't get over how many guys were totally fawning over me.

"Hey hot stuff, never seen you around here before, you new?" A boy asked me. He smelled like cheap body spray, but I wasn't entirely put off by it. I took a sip from my drink, and played with the cherry stem in my fingertips.

"Yeah I guess you could say that. I'm Kayla." Before I knew it, I was swaying my ass on the dance floor with this stranger. I wanted to have *fun*! And Trey was pretty cool. At one point, he placed his hands on my hips and swayed with me. I was feeling it... and I could also feel my pussy warming up from his touch.

"Hey, like, uh..." I started to protest, but Trey spun me around, his commanding hand cupping my ass through my thin dress fabric. He dipped me down, leaned in close and I could feel his stubble brush against my soft chin as he pressed his lips into mine. I brought a hand up to his chiseled face and pressed into it, reveling in the taste of him, hormones surging through my body. No, this is wrong. You're a man. Get out of here.

I realized what was happening. A small pop escaped between our mouths as I pulled away, with me still staring in awe and shock and wonder into his eyes. "Sorry," I mouthed. I scampered on my heels through the crowd, letting the club door swing wide open as I dashed to my car.

I kicked off my shoes and stormed right into Scott's workshop. "Hey! HEY!" I yelled, waking him up. His head was on his desk, messy with papers and figures and drawings, with his remote right next to him.

"Oh, K-Kayla? What's wrong?"

"*You're* wrong, dummy! You made me like, act like some straight girl! I'm not a girl!" I clenched my fists, and I was seething with anger. I had to be mad, that was the only thing I felt was grounding me to my masculinity at this point. Scott looked frustrated at this.

"I don't know who you *were*, I've only known you as this chick that keeps insisting on being a guy again. I don't even know how this remote could have ever changed you into a girl. It's a *mind control* remote. I went over my notes over and over, there's nothing in here about changing bodies."

No, that's impossible. I'm a guy. I've always been a guy. A guy named... Greg. I clumped my hair in my hands and sat on the couch.

"Maybe..." Scott offered. "Maybe the remote made you think you used to be a guy?"

"Even if that's true, why would you like, keep making me girlier?" I realized I had started to cry.

"To make it easier for you, I guess." He held the remote in his hand, pondering. "I think you'll be happier if you give in to it, Kayla."

"Don't call me that!" I yelped, half choking on my tears. "I'm a *man*!" Scott raised his arm and pointed the remote at me, pressing the big red button. "What..." I sniffled, wiping my wet eyes with the back of my finger. "What did you do?"

Scott sat next to me, placing the remote back on the table. He put his arm around me to comfort me, and it was kinda nice to feel his warmth. I rested my head on his shoulder, and hugged my knees up against my chest as my emotions got the better of me. "I took away those dreams you've been having, Kayla. You should feel much better now."

"Dreams, what dreams?" I asked, my tears finally drying up. Scott was nice enough to rub my back for me. He smiled, "Don't worry about it anymore. Hey, we should get some sleep, it's late and you partied pretty hard tonight."

I giggled. Yeah I did. I thought back to that cute boy from earlier, and felt a little naughty for having kissed him. Even the memory of the way his tongue felt against mine on the dance floor made my toes curl in excitement.

"Yeah, you're right. I'm sleepy..." I didn't have to tell him about Trey, besides, Scott knew I was a bad girl. I didn't have to give him *all* the details.

I stood and stretched, giving him a full view of my panties under my slutty little dress. His eyes dropped, and I had his full attention. Smirking, I sashayed to the bedroom, my tiny little ass leading the way. I knew what I was in for, and I wanted his dick in me so badly after that hot night of dancing on Trey's crotch against my pussy. Maybe tomorrow night I'll go find that boy again, give him a wild night he'll never forget.

XX

BEAN

TAGS: THE AUTHOR, EMILY, BEAN

We named our unborn baby Bean. We scheduled regular visits with doctors and did all we could do to prepare for the coming months. Check. We bought the books. Check. We went to classes. Check. Emily ate healthy and exercised regularly, with special consideration to her figure and her strength for when it came time to somehow literally magically push a wriggly crying creature that would weigh 8 or so pounds out the bottom of her body and expect to leave the hospital in one piece. Check.

We stopped going to therapy. Who had time for that now? And besides, wasn't this the thing we wanted? The thing that was keeping our marriage from being perfectly in sync? Now we had The Project: the thing to work towards together that would reconnect the broken bonds of our relationship, the thing that was the foundation of so many couples before us.

Parenthood.

I felt I had a pretty good idea of parenthood. Feed and love Bean, and eventually Bean grows up. Maybe Bean likes you, maybe Bean doesn't. I also knew what I didn't love about parenthood. I had that mental list of things my parents had done filed away in the back of my brain labeled *Trauma*.

So, do the good things and avoid the bad things. Got it. Easy. There's lists and resources available for that.

The season changed and I watched as Emily changed, too. Bean grew into a bump. Our confidence grew and we sent out notices to friends and family. We made a Facebook post and received hundreds of likes and messages from people we haven't talked to in ages. We were actually having a baby! This was exciting! Check check check.

We went to get an ultrasound. We told the technician we didn't want to know the sex. We got to hear Bean's heartbeat and see it wriggling on the monitor. Emily and I stared at it with cosmic curiosity. How did this happen? How are we deserving of such magic?

"You're sure you don't want to know?" The technician said, as she pointed definitively to the infinitesimally small appendage affixed to the small helpless creature on camera. She was bad at her job.

It was a boy!

You know the story: time speeds up when a baby is on the horizon.

Dates come faster when you know how to count down the days. When there is certainty attached. A predictable outcome. A result of carefully planned science, predictive models, routine best-practices carried out by interested parties. We had a checklist and we followed it. Bean's probably going to be a Capricorn. Expect baby showers thrown by other people who would decorate with lots of blue. Notify employers that you'll be gone for a while, but not *too* long because you live in America. Oh, and you need to pick a real name for Bean. And probably start using his pronouns.

We felt pretty good about it all. Our house was clean, we had made the plans, now all we had to do was relax and wait for Emily's water to break.

Her water broke. Check.

This was happiness, right?

We rushed to the hospital, carrying the weight of our hearts with us.

Finally, I thought, we've reached The Moment that would make all the pain worth it. All the arguments were a thing of the past, we had a new lease on life. I'd finally be able to move past those stories. There would be no room left in my world for that stuff.

After all, I was going to be a dad.

I watched as Emily struggled against the tidal forces that now compelled her body to shift in phases. Struggling to get comfortable, waiting for The Moment when all the doctors and nurses would rush in and complete their little checklists and write on the whiteboards and tell you to push. I watched as she lay, bearing the full brunt of her nature as our parents had done for us. Fully exposed and beautiful. A real human in childbirth, experiencing the kind of helplessness where the gap between worlds opens and one is called to push back against it.

She touched humanity. A rite of passage that wasn't mine to have.

Push.

He's here. He's incredible. You did great.

To say that time slowed down is wrong.

Time stopped.

Check.

POTENTIAL

TAGS: THE AUTHOR, BEAN, KAYLA

You have to raise a baby without knowing who they will become. Is the baby going to be a good person? Will they be successful? Will they be healthy? Happy? Can we keep them safe? How long will it take to realize their potential? What will we be like when they get there? Do we really have to raise this kid for years, without knowing what kind of kid we're in for?

I'm holding my tiny infant in the crook of my arm as it wanes in and out of sleep. It just wants to be held. It's my shift, so Emily is asleep for the next three hours. I try to imagine what kind of person I might be in five, ten, twenty, forty years. I try to picture my child having children. I try to imagine myself as a grandfather. I try to imagine myself being old at all.

I get warm fuzzy feelings looking at my newborn, all wrapped in snuggly cloth. I try to imagine what he dreams of, having had no experience to draw on. He's only now arrived from the dark nothingness of pre-existence, only to be dressed in snuggly cloth with cute penguins on it. As far as I know, he has no concept of time, of place, of self. Just eat, sleep, poop.

Sounds nice.

I take a moment to congratulate myself for not logging into Tumblr for the last five days to write a story, or talk to anyone as... her. I've finally found my place, which is here. I'm a dad! This is my son, and he's so tiny and wonderful and I'm looking forward to seeing him grow up. To be the cool dad that I wanted my dad to be. Perhaps be the person that Dad wanted himself to be. I suppose he was fine, in the end. He loved me, I loved him, it got complicated. He made some mistakes, sure, but I've mostly forgiven him now that he's been gone for a few years. But I am not him. I won't make the same mistakes he did. Not with Bean.

I frown. That feeling is back. That sad, dark feeling of longing again. It radiates through my body and leaves me restless. I glance at my phone on the desk. The light of the screen casts shadows of everything in the after-midnight dim of my living room.

I hate myself.

Bean is fast asleep. I shake my head. Don't open the app. I've uninstalled that app five times before and somehow, I keep coming back to it. Why am I like this? I have a baby, I'm not like this. I'm not an addict. I'm not some awful creep that would look at porn images on his phone while holding his infant son, I'm a good person. I have a wife, a home, a job, a child. I have everything!

Kayla Hey everyone, I'm back! Sorry for disappearing. Life's been so busy haha.

Doesn't she know how delicate everything is? Does Kayla recognize that my wife would leave me if she discovered that I looked at porn all the time, wrote these stories, pretended to be a woman online? She'd take Bean from me, her family would abandon me, my friends would question me. I'd be left with nothing. I have no family to turn to.

I've built all of this, and yet I can't get Kayla out of my fucking head.

"You can quit anytime, you know." Kayla said. She's posed like a pin-up model wearing a red and white polka dot dress, sheer nude leggings, and shimmery red pumps on her non-feet. Her face is still missing, a blur that I can't focus on.

I've tried quitting. I tried quitting when I moved to Seattle. I tried when I got married. But it only got worse. I tried when we bought the house, and now I have a child. An amazing child.

"Maybe you don't want to quit? What's so wrong with writing? I thought you liked writing." Kayla said. She changes her position, leaning towards the camera, her non-hands on her non-hips with a sassy 'come-and-get-me' look on her non-smirk.

I do like writing. I like the way people respond to it; the way I can make people feel things with words alone. But I want to be able to share my writing with others, not hide it like this.

"This isn't just about the writing, is it?"

No? Yes? It doesn't matter, because there's no way I can talk about this with Emily, it would break her heart. She'd leave me, I know it. How would I explain that to anyone?

"Well, I'm having fun. I get to write some stories, talk about my life, and share myself with friends. I get to flirt and be sexy. I'm a girl forever in my 20s with a fun and fulfilling sex life."

You wasted *my* entire 20s.

She actually laughed. "It wasn't that bad, was it?"

And what about Bean? He can't grow up with a dad that is stuck on his phone all the time living another life.

"Why not? Have you seen another parent out there that didn't have their noses in their phones while their kid craved their attention? You think people aren't always seeking a means of escaping their chaotic lives with the tools they find lying around them at the time? Where do you think their heads are at? No one lives in only one place. Anyway, I have this great idea for a story, it's about a guy who turns into a girl but like, it's unclear if he actually wants it or not, and—"

I can't keep doing this. You can't control me.

"You're right, but I'm afraid you have no choice. At least I know who I am and have the words to describe it. One day you'll realize you can't talk without me."

THE WAKING HOURS

Focus on something else.

Focus on Bean!

It feels good to focus on someone else's checklist for once.

Caring for others is self-care.

And my, how the days fly by.

One-week check-up.

One-month check-up.

Three-month check-up.

First laugh.

Back to work.

Focus.

Rolling over.

Sitting up.

Six-month check-up.

Time for the monthly photo to post to Facebook.

He's getting so big!

Nine-month check-up.

Focus. Focus.

Is he standing up yet?

256

Find a daycare.

Time to get larger diapers.

Time to take out the diaper garbage.

Cook food again.

Focus, damn it!

Can he eat solids yet?

Time to plan a first birthday party, already?

Such a fun age.

THE QUIET HOURS

TAGS: THE AUTHOR, EMILY, KAYLA, UNWILLING, SEX

At a certain point, parenting became easier as Emily and I settled into autopilot. Everything was scheduled, everything fit within a daily strategy. Any deviation from the routine would disrupt the delicate balance and our house would burn down. We'd never admit that, though.

In the quiet hours—when we had them—we'd regroup to take inventory, assess the damage, and prepare to rejoin the battle again tomorrow. Emily would look in the mirror at her post-pregnancy body and feel sad. I'd look in the mirror and see:

My beard was scraggly, I was greasy. I felt unattractive, disgusting.

Somewhere along the way, I got fat.

Guess I neglected to care for myself.

"Why don't you want to fuck me?" I'm brought into the present as I see Emily staring at me, toothbrush in hand. She's upset that she has to say it out loud, who knows how long she's been holding onto the feeling. I haven't been feeling very sexy, and I didn't realize she even wanted sex tonight. Or the previous night.

[[Or the night before that.]]

Ugh, shut up, Kayla. She knew what was eating away at me. Every ounce of me went into managing the child, my marriage, my job, and Kayla. I had no energy left.

I sat up in bed, attentive, phone on its face. "I'm just tired, is all. I don't mean to make it a thing. Do you want to have sex now?"

"Yeah, but I want you to help me feel sexy too. You never flirt with me, you never ask to fuck me. You don't make me feel wanted. Why?"

[[Yeah, why is that, lover-boy? You never have a problem writing your little stories. Can't you man up and fuck her like we get fucked online?]]

"I'm sorry, I'll do better." I lied.

I summoned the energy she wanted me to have, and gave her a comforting hug and a sweet kiss on the neck. She's clearly still mad, rolling her eyes and letting me fumble my way through this. She wants me to prove that I still love her. With a sigh, she takes off her pants and underwear and crawls into bed. I unbuckle my belt and get undressed in front of her. I feel large. She looks sad and gets into the sex-having position. It's as unsexy as it gets.

I start, and it's heartless. The air is stale, the room is cold. The only sounds are the soft creaking of the fibers in the new mattress we got at IKEA, the dry rubbing of genital skin.

[[Is this the best you can do? Don't you know how to have sex any other way? Look at her face, she's bored. You're fucking boring. Remember that time that stranger online told you to suck his cock, and you did it? Where's that person now? Are you even enjoying this? Are you getting tired already? You're still soft. Stay with me, try to imagine how you'd like to get fucked if you were her. If you had her pussy. If you had some big man like you fondling your breasts, touching your butt, destroying your cunt, devouring you. Isn't that better? Look, you're getting into a better rhythm. Keep going, you're doing great. What if you pretend that she's hypnotized into loving you? Into being the perfect housewife? Or that she used to be some guy who—]]

Stop.

[[She wants this! You *have* to fuck her. You don't want her to think you're a loser husband, do you? If this is the only way you can make it work, then why not lean into it? Fuck her, harder! That's what she wants, isn't it? That's what she wants! In, out. In, out. You know what to do. Treat yourself like one of the brainless girls from the stories, This is what you would want, that's what gets you off, right? To be fucked like a girl?]]

"Stop! Please!" Emily yells.

I freeze. Refocus. The world returns to me. I look into her eyes, soft and scared.

"I'm... sorry. I'm really sorry."

XXX

White Knight

Emily was a daydreamer.

She and her sister lived in a pressure cooker, a family of achievers. Her parents were entrepreneurs, educators, scientists, and her younger sister was similarly ruthlessly ambitious. They had relatives in high places, and lived in neat, tidy homes. Despite their shiny and competent family exterior, there were plenty of struggles.

Her father was a high-functioning alcoholic, and drank to cure himself of his frustrating absent-mindedness. He would frequently give glasses of wine to his daughters claiming it was sophisticated and European. Her sister was his protégé, the golden child who saw things the way he did and could do no wrong. Her mother, a child of the military, enabled all of this so long as their household was clean and unbroken.

Poor Emily, soft-spoken, thin and fragile Emily. Head-in-the-clouds Emily who was often a bit starry-eyed, clumsy, who felt it hard to concentrate on math. Gentle Emily who wanted to read books and spend time in nature to memorize the names of different species of native plants.

She didn't get the kind of validation she wanted from her family, who taught her she wasn't worth anything if she wasn't perfectly orderly. So, eventually, she started seeing a man much older than her. A man who told her she was beautiful, confident, and strong. A man who had multiple girlfriends and children. A man who groomed her with whiskey sours. A man who, one night, broke her.

She didn't tell her family.

So it was time for college, and she decided to get as far away from home as she could manage. She picked a school in New York. She dated around and found men that liked how attractive she was. She had come into her womanhood well-versed in sex and understood what it took to get men to like her.

She wondered if she'd ever find a guy who was just nice. A guy who would treat her well and with respect. Someone handsome and intelligent. A white knight. Then, she met a boy from New Jersey at an improv workshop.

They got along really well. He was wholesome and patient. He offered to do favors for her. He was tall, handsome, and ambitious. He didn't drink, he was sober, he was in control. She was so smitten with him, but he was clearly a little shy about it. She knew what she wanted, though. She wanted to feel unbroken. So she kissed him first.

They decided to move in together. He had lots of friends and brought her to fun places. They took a road trip across the country, and landed in a cute little apartment in Seattle.

He got down on one knee in front of her in a snowy clearing on a ski slope in Leavenworth. There were snowflakes melting on his reddened cheeks, the sun was warm. It's perfect. It's the two of them against the world. They're in love. She says yes. They cry.

They got good jobs, and she was close to her family again. This time, it's different. Her younger sister has moved far away, and Emily got to feel like the responsible one in her parents' lives. Finally, they can be proud of her. She's done the hard work: improved herself, found the man, gotten pregnant, and started a family of her own where she sets the rules and surrounds herself with the kindness and comforts of her choosing.

Except there was something wrong with her white knight.

He was a little secretive. Sometimes he stayed awake too long into the night, or spent too much time in the bathroom. Sometimes the sex was great, other times they couldn't seem to connect. He's always on his phone.

She wondered if he was cheating on her. She didn't know what she had done to deserve it. They shared everything together.

One night, though, he lost control. He was lost in another world.

She yelled out: *"Stop! Please!"*

They've already tried couple's therapy, but he only became more and more depressed. They struggled with intimacy in the quiet hours, and her past trauma was dragging her down deeper. She finally sought therapy for herself to address her painful past and her frustrating relationship with her spouse. Her therapist helped her dig into her emotional and sexual needs. Emily told them that she and her husband are hurting. They're broken. She's not sure what to do.

"Well, have you tried asking him what turns him on?"

Gradual, Instant

Reader, we have already explored what it means for a TG story to be realistic, magical, willing, or unwilling. Whether the central character has any agency in their transformation, and which method is used to achieve the final result. In the end, they all become girls. But there exists another important axis in these stories: Time. Whether or not the transformation happens instantly and quickly, or slowly and gradually.

Gradual transformations usually involve the subject experiencing bodily changes in several stages. They notice skin texture changes, they lose body hair, their hair grows out to a stereotypically feminine style, their body shape adjusts to meet the standard. This happens over days or weeks, or maybe the author can describe the transformation taking place over minutes but with such tantalizing detail that it feels like eternity. The focus is on the experience of the change itself, which allows the subject (and ultimately, you, the reader) to process how it feels to change in real time.

Instant transformations get you straight to the meat of the story. The subject is quickly transformed, and it's what happens *after* the transformation that forms the foundation of the narrative.

I have written a lot of instant transformation stories, as evidenced by this book. My stories also usually feature magic and unwilling participants.

It wasn't enough to change boys into girls. Changing someone's entire world in a flash allows the story to spiral into nightmarish torture as the victim's entire former personality is completely erased. It wasn't enough that the subject was unwilling to change at first. They had to have their identity eradicated so that we could pretend that they enjoyed the transformation at all. They could forget that they were ever somebody to begin with. They could exist as a new person in the world as their tormentor designed them to be.

They are now simply women, absent from the memory of their former life.

I was so willfully ignorant to what any transformation might mean for myself that I couldn't help but use this same formula over and over again. The characters I wrote meant nothing to me, they could have whatever names or backgrounds I could think of. It didn't matter. By the end, I wanted to watch their perfect little worlds burn to the ground so that a new character could be reborn from the ashes. Not dead, not even truly changed. Reincarnated. A fresh start.

Gradual transformations, however, are far too real for me. That's *real* change. That's the kind of change with consequences and pain, the sort that you have to work through every day. To sit and take time with your changes means you have to feel your emotions and learn and grow from the experience. That's *hard*.

In the gender transformation erotica writing world, there's plenty of stolen and borrowed faces and bodies of women to accommodate each story. They are there to help your imagination run wild. It's pornographic, they are there to help you get off in the indulgent fantasy.

But for me—it was about the words. It wasn't ever really about the sex, or the photos, it was always about using the words to bring *myself* to life. I used them as a means of escaping the reality that all I wanted was a fresh start. A blank page. I would trade everything I had to be reborn, with no memory of my former life.

I wanted to forget that I was capable of feeling this way about the life I had built, about all the people I loved.

I wanted my perfect little world to burn to the ground.

[[IRRESISTIBLE]]

TAGS: TG, MAGIC, POTION, KAYLA

"Come sit next to me, Kayla."

"Fuck you, that's not my name!" The girl shook her head and gave an awkward smile after a pause. "But I'll be Kayla for you if you want, stud."

"Be nice, Kayla. We can't have a pretty girl like you with a dirty mouth like that."

She steamed. "Asshole, I'll get you for this... but I thought you wanted me to be your dirty girl?" She blinked her eyelashes at me and pulled a hair aside from her face.

"Oh, you'll be a dirty girl alright. I'm glad the potion is kicking in. You'll feel much better after it takes full effect."

"No... I won't let you! I can't stop... thinking about how great your cock would taste right now." She sidled up to me and reached her dainty hand into my pants, taking hold of my dick.

"You don't have to think about it, darling. Look at you, you are already oozing femininity and sex. All you needed was that extra push. Give in."

Her hand tenses on my dick. "I'm going to make you pay for this... after I suck you dry, baby." She dipped her head onto

268

my throbbing member and took it into her mouth. After a few minutes of lustful sucking, she brought her mischievous gaze to meet mine.

"Mmmm, I think he's finally gone, lover boy. Can we fuck already?"

XXXX

The Question

TAGS: THE AUTHOR, EMILY, KAYLA

"What turns you on?"

To be asked this question so directly was an event so catastrophic that the formless void around me shook and tore and exploded into form. The empty black became black. The world shifted and blurred as this interrogation brought with it a dreadful beast with razor sharp fangs. It was a hunter, eyes laser-focused on my answer as prey. Its presence demanded that I feed the apocalypse. I am commanded to use my muscles enough to receive and filter and expel air, and move my lips to deliver its meal of truth in response. The horror called on me to reach an arm into the dark place of my heart to draw out the justification and meaning for my existence. To quell the predator, I'd have to deliver my soul.

[[You're so dramatic.]]

"What turns me on?" I repeated the question back to Emily, who stood silently in nervous anticipation. This wasn't a question asked to be sexy or charming, this was a question expressed out of concern. She wanted an answer. She needed an answer.

Kayla's there, too, of course. Tight jeans, cute shoes, red blouse with ruffles, hoop earrings, a dark streak of void covers her non-face.

[[Yeah, what turns you on, tough guy?]]

"Uh, well, I kinda like cute or sexy outfits on girls."

[[Yeah, I do wear those things pretty often, don't I.]]

"I like when... I get to feel your whole body, I like when you come out of the shower, and you're wet and smooth and freshly shaved."

She does have a nice body.

[[I'm jealous.]]

Jealous?

[[Yeah, that sounds right. What does she see in you, again? Your personality? Why is this so hard for you? Go ahead, tell her all about me. That should answer the question pretty quickly.]]

Why is she even asking this question? Does she really need therapy? I thought we had sex figured out. Penis goes in, penis goes out. I cum, she cums. We move on with our life.

[[Yeah, but you *know* it's way more than that, babe. It's body parts in mouths, it's things in other things, it's messy and sloppy and wild and untamed. It's uninhibited pleasure seekers going bananas on each other until they start missing deadlines, pushing away the limitations of the world they've slotted themselves neatly into. It's giving into disgusting carnal desires with yourself or another person or multiple other persons until you finally peel away the outer shell and reveal the pure untouched golden core of your soul.]]

Why can't I be normal?

[[I don't know the answer to that. What's normal?]]

A person with a job, a wife, a kid, a person who knows their place in the world and can navigate it until they die.

[[Haven't you tried that? Haven't you *done* that? Have you considered that you don't want to be normal? Have you considered that you might want to be me?]]

A sex-starved nymphomaniac with a hundred different faces that lies to people and posts depressing stories about turning men into girls?

[[No, silly. I don't write the stories, you do. You always have. Why do you think you write the stories?]]

I don't know, I feel like I've always written them. Whenever I get sad or horny or lonely, I write or think about writing. Whenever I think about myself, I instead think about writing these characters and bringing them to life. And I want to feel those feelings with other people who maybe feel the same way I do, so I share them.

[[Or have incredible cybersex with random guys.]]

That's different, that's—

[[Let's face it. You're a mess. You barely exist. You're aging in a vacuum, alone. You see your dad in the mirror more and more and you hate yourself for it. You're getting nowhere with your relationship, so you give up and resolve yourself to doing this forever. You lie, you hide, you obscure the truth in shame. This is your so-called life, and while you're not dead yet, you may as well be. Which leaves one question.]]

Don't say it.

[[Have you considered admitting that you just want to be a woman?]]

[[THE CAVE]]

TAGS: TG, MAGIC, MOUNTAIN, SEX, DOOR

Exhausted, our party pressed onward. Up and up and up, through lush jungles and through clear valleys with unbroken views of this magical region. It was a two week trek through more difficult terrain than I'd ever seen.

But today was the day we would finally summit Mt Kintarr.

As a researcher, I wanted to learn everything I could about this place. Since it was my team's first visit here, all I knew was that it was dangerous. Several hikers were reported missing over the past few years. My team and I were nothing but cautious, and hopeful to track down some of the causes of the disappearances.

But up and up and up we went. Until we came upon a cave in the mountainside. The air was fresh and cold and crisp.

I peered into the darkness of the deep cave. This was an odd place for a cave, I thought. My partners were equally perplexed. I took a step inside, and my eyes adjusted to the dark within. It wasn't as deep as I thought…

"A door?"

I turned back to my colleagues, who shrugged. A simple wooden door was sitting in a flat section of the cave wall. There was a simple handle, and nothing else of note around it.

"Who the hell puts a door here?" Skeptical, I placed my hand on the handle and gave it a jiggle. To my surprise, it turned easily and creaked as I opened it to peer inside.

A hallway? Long and narrow, with a second door at the other side! I could hear the faint sound of music playing in the distance.

I journeyed on, into the hallway. Walking, walking, walking. The walls were plain, and it was dim. The music grew louder as I got closer. I put my hand on the doorknob, turned it, and stepped inside.

"Heyyy!" A crowd of young partiers cheered as I set foot inside. I was taken aback! This looked like some kind of college party? But... we're in the middle of a mountain range!

A tall guy approached me, smiling wide. "Welcome to the party, newbie! I'm sure you have a million questions. I'm Omar."

"Uhh, yeah, I—" I started, but choked a little on my voice. It sounded high pitched, but maybe that was the loud music? I cleared my throat and tried again. "I'm..." my voice cracked. I put a hand to my throat, and was equally startled to not feel my beard. It was gone? Like I had recently freshly shaved, but there was no coarseness at all!

My eyes drifted to my chest, my arms, my legs, my feet. What was I wearing? I had... breasts?! Oh fuck, I'm a girl!?

"What the fuck? What the *fuck*?" I yelled. Omar put a hand on my shoulder.

"As I said. A million questions. Let's start with an easy one, but try to relax. What's your name?"

I was going to lose it. But Omar seemed to know what was going on. "I'm Penelope." I paused. "No, I'm Penelope. What the hell? I'm Penelope!"

"Nice to meet you, Penelope. Like I said, I'm Omar. I can't tell you any other name, because that's who I am. Isn't that right?"

"Uhh…" I started, freaking out more, grasping at my long brown hair. "Yes, I'm definitely Penelope, I'm a 21 year old girl getting my bachelor's degree in art school." I continued, dismayed, "From Madison, Wisconsin, my parents are Roy and Stephanie Almeyer, I have an orange cat named Tickles, and what the fuck is happening?"

Omar casually turned and looked at the other partiers, who were having a great time hanging out and chatting. Some of them waved at me. "We are all like this, Penelope. I don't understand it, either. But I've been here for 43 years, I think, and haven't aged a day. Ricky over there thinks we might be dead. I think we're all dreaming. Sasha is convinced the cave entrance is a portal to a weird pocket universe, but I think she's full of shit."

I turned and looked at the door, still anxiously feeling the foreign curves of my young body as if that would somehow calm me down. My dick was… gone. I could even feel that I had a whole different reproductive system. I moved differently.

"I know what you're thinking. Maybe if you leave you can go back to normal. And maybe you can, but we don't know what happens when someone leaves. They certainly never come back."

"What?" I looked back at him.

"Oh, we've had a few people try it. Some people can't take it the instant they get here, and they walk back out. A few have promised – and I mean *promised* – that they would only take one single step out that door and come back inside to let us know what they saw. But, they never came back." He lit up a cigarette, and offered it to me. I waved it off.

"I decided, 'fuck it,' I'm staying. I never even got to see the view from the top of the mountain."

My brain was reeling. 43 years? Never aging? Part of me wondered if Omar was telling the truth, or if he was like me. Not actually a tall man named Omar. Just like how I'm not actually a petite brunette girl named Penelope from Wisconsin.

I kept my eye on the door, waiting for when my crew would arrive. Who they might become, if I'd even recognize them. Minutes, then hours passed. No one came through the door. Did they even follow me? Did it matter?

The party went on without me, no doubt because everyone here had seen this play out before. A stupefied outsider that would either run and never return – or give in to the change and become a willing participant.

I had to make a decision.

I waited long enough for my tears to dry up. I stood, turned around, and decided to at least make an effort to get to know some of the people waiting for me to join in.

***

Six or so months later

"So, Penelope was it?" The new guy asked me again.

I twirled my hair and blew a bubble from my bubblegum. A little bored of this guy already. "Yeah."

"And you mean that you've *always* been a girl named Penelope? Like... I've always been... a guy... named... R-Roger?"

"Look, Roger, the sooner you give in to it the easier it'll be for you — and all of us. Now, do you want a drink or not?"

It had been a few months and I had started getting into a routine. I always kept an eye on that exit door, but wasn't brave enough to take it on. Instead, I found myself relaxing into my new body, my new self. I mean, I was *hot*. Some of the guys and girls here agreed that I might be one of the top few hottest girls in the cave.

And one month ago, I finally gave in to my body's own sexual needs. I was a woman, now, after all.

Jake had been gentle with me. He was patient, kind, humble, and a little awkward. He was good-looking for a man, even though I hadn't been attracted to men.

But after months and months of awkward masturbating in my bedroom, I started realizing I could probably handle it. I had

278

gotten pretty used to my vagina, feeling and understanding its shape and needs with every session. I must have spent an entire day fingering and studying it when I wasn't feeling like socializing. It wasn't like there was much else to do.

I could probably handle a cock. After all, I used to have one.

And with Jake, I hadn't been all that awkward around him. Even though I couldn't tell him the truth about my past, I didn't try to either. He may have even thought I was a different sort of girl in my past life, too. Not that it mattered.

I brought him to my room.

We undressed.

It was my first time seeing another man naked for me, presenting themselves for me. I certainly wasn't a gay man, but I knew I had different needs now. Maybe my tastes could adapt, too.

I felt his musculature as he felt mine. His caress felt amazing on my skin, having not been touched intimately by anyone for months. I took the first step and kissed him, feeling his dick press against my tummy. I leaned in closer, feeling his warmth as he squeezed my butt. I had never felt like this before. So loved, so cherished, so wanted, so vulnerable.

He tasted great. We swapped saliva as he moved to firmly squishing my breasts, a move I knew all too well. It felt fucking fantastic, and it only made me hornier.

Gone were my inhibitors, the tie to reality keeping me from embracing womanhood. Gone was the guilt of not living my past truth anymore. Gone was all the doubt that I could be sexy, girlish, beautiful.

I kissed his neck, his chest, his belly button. Before I knew it, my lust had fully absorbed me and I had his whole strong, musky cock in my mouth. Teasing it, testing it, tasting it. I wanted to learn all I could about being a pretty girl, the object of a man (or woman's desires). I knew that I had to play the part if I was to have a fulfilling life in the cave.

I could only give him head for so long, so I looked up at him and practically begged with my eyes. So he lifted me up, grabbed me, picked me up, took me to the bed, dropped me down, spread my legs, and inserted his meaty member into my deliriously wet clit. He pushed and pushed and pushed and pushed until I felt my whole being filled to the brim. I felt so immensely full of him, my eyes rolled to the back of my head and I automatically let out a satisfied chirp. That chirp became a low moan, then panting as he repeatedly fucked me.

He'd done this before, I thought. He knew exactly what he was doing. The lucky son of a bitch must have also been a man in his prior life, I thought. There was no way a 'new' guy could be this fucking good at fucking.

He was the first, but definitely not the last guy I'd ride.

***

Six or so years later

"Heyyy!" I cheered with my crew as two new people emerged from the Mystery Door. I always LOVED new people.

If they stayed, I almost always got to fuck them—guy or girl. I had definitely built up quite a reputation over the years.

"Uhhh..." the short cute girl started. "Where are we... wait... why am I...!?" She frazzled as she marveled at her body, her hands, her voice. The tall boy was equally perplexed.

I rolled my eyes. Always SO predictable. At least she was pretty, and it had been a while since I had a girl-on-girl night... I gave my canned speech to help them acclimate.

"We, um, looking for the body of Dr. Wrexley... he uh... went missing six and a half years ago. Have you seen him?"

I hadn't heard that name in a long time! Too bad I couldn't tell them it was me, not that I cared anymore. I learned to love being sweet little sexy Penelope. One of my many boyfriends, Derek, squeezed my ass as he walked over to check on the new people. He was my go-to when I wanted to rough-house in the sack, and boy did he deliver! I gave him a naughty look and a quick peck on the cheek and smacked his ass right back before answering the question.

"No." I said plainly, before posing a little to show off my assets. "But I'm Penelope. What's your name, sweetheart?"

"Cl...Claire. Wait, that's... my name?"

I licked my lips. She looked so fine. But I guessed she didn't know how to use her body... yet. I sauntered closer, close enough to see her nervous sweat forming. I took her hand, leaned into her ear, letting my breasts graze hers as I whispered "I can help you feel better. Teach you a few things you might really like."

281

Shy, confused, and more than a bit aroused, she followed me without another word to my chamber. She looked back at the tall boy, who was still reeling from the experience. I was thinking I might come back to him later... for seconds.

***

Seventy-five or so years later

Sigh. So many people come and gone. The party at the cave was still going strong, and little old me was still as slutty as ever. I had had so many partners I'd lost count, adrift in a sea of cocks and cunts (though I'd eventually grow to prefer dicks, they were always so reliable, and the men so eager to worship me).

Roger didn't last long at all, leaving during a mental break-down. But not before I teased him endlessly.

Claire became as wild and cock-hungry as I was, and was my best friend and confidante for many years. She eventually decided to take the exit door, though, thinking maybe she would return to the real world as a new woman. I cried a lot that year.

Omar left early, which was a shame because he was prob-ably the best fuck I've ever had. He decided it was finally 'his time.'

Jake once punched one of the other girls in the cave, forced her to leave, and after years of bitterness and assholery he finally took the exit. It was bittersweet watching my first real boyfriend go under such awful circumstances.

So that left me. The Senior. Another lifetime, this time as a forever young and impossibly hot and sexually charged woman. I didn't forget my past life, but at a certain point my time in here surpassed the time I'd ever spent as a man.

I put on my sexiest lingerie, my hottest dress, did my makeup and hair, put on my cutest earrings, strapped on my fiercest heels, and went to the party in style.

I made the rounds, saying hi to everyone I was friends with. Savoring the moment as I swayed a little to the music, dancing with my boys and girls. Moving closer to the door.

When no one was looking, I took a deep breath, turned the door handle, opened it wide, stepped out, and—

XXXXXXXXXXXXXXXXXXXXXXXXXXXXXXXXX

Confrontation

Quiet.

With the exception of the dull throbbing in my head, and the gentle sounds of Emily sleeping soundly next to me. I roll over and check my phone.

It's 2 in the morning.

I hated how much sense she made.

I hated how stupid I felt.

"I liked that last story." Kayla said, leaning against the wall. "What's on the other side of the door?" Her body casts shadows, the soft red glow from the alarm clock on the nightstand illuminating her dress. Her face peeks out from under the waves of her hair. She's smiling.

I don't know, Kayla. I'm going through some things.

"That's alright. We have each other. Can't sleep?"

No.

She kneels at my bedside and folds her arms over the sheets so her face is level with mine. I can see the reflection of the moon outside in her pupils. "Well, I have some more writing ideas if you want to go over them. Or maybe we could check in on some people and see if they're in a flirting mood, or maybe—"

Why do you look like that?

"Huh? Why do I look like what?"

You're a red-head.

"Hm. Suppose I am. I mean, you made me. I'm you, remember?"

Yeah, but I look nothing like you. You're tiny. You're fashionable. You have all this self-esteem. You're my dream woman. You're nothing like me. If I'm supposed to want to be a woman, as you say, there's no reasonable way I can ever look like you.

"Sure, but that's why we live in different places, right? I do my thing, you do yours. We're partners. We keep each other in check. You want to be a woman, so you get to be me on the Internet!"

We're incompatible.

"What do you mean by that? We don't exist without each other."

We live in these different places, but neither of us gets to leave. Face it: you're not happy either. You're not an outlet or an escape—you're a prisoner. You don't get to show your face, despite touting how much you love to share your joy with people. Even if the sex is miserable for me, it's not even real for you. You say you know what you like, but you've never truly experienced anything. You've built up this false impression of the real world as much as I have, and as long as I suffer, you suffer. You're as oblivious and unhappy as I am.

"Well... how do we fix this?"

We aren't the same person. I can't be you, and you don't *want* to be me. We're two completely different people. So you're right. Maybe I do want to be a woman. Fuck.

"Okay, awesome. And how is that supposed to work? You're going to confess everything to Emily, walk out on her? What? You don't know the first thing about being a woman. That's why you have me! So why even attempt it? You'd really choose to lose everything that you've built in your life for that?"

I don't know what else would fix it. I can't stop thinking about these fucking stories.

So what does it mean? If we can't be the same person, then what are we protecting ourselves from becoming?

Who are we?

Who am I?

Well?

Kayla?

The Storm

"Fuck."

All at once I'm hit with the familiar scent of saltwater. My toes wriggled in the soft, warm fabric socks on my feet. My lungs gaped and sucked the heavy air in, before easing back to push it back out. It's cold but not unforgiving. I gazed out at the pink and purple sky over the ocean horizon, over the deck of a great ship, through a girl's eyes that absorbed every drop of light from the sunset.

This wasn't supposed to happen. I grabbed a small section of the soft flesh on my forearm and pinched, hoping to dispel the illusion. The sharp pain erupted from my veins as they were obstructed, and reminded me that *No, this isn't a dream.* Not one that could be escaped, anyway.

I took two careful steps towards the edge of the ship and looked down into the deep, deep waters below. The swirling mass of porn surged and raged against the siding, battling it and testing its resilience and strength. Testing my resolve.

"Kayla!"

A crash of water slammed the rig and rode along its planks. It spilled out over the deck, knocking me over and sliding me with it. My body slammed against the wall. Tired muscles and flesh and bone caught the impact and I spasmed. With effort, I rose to my feet and staggered to the lines, taking one in hand, and pulling as a leaf in the wind to align the bow against the waves. I grit my teeth as the blisters in my hand caught the finer fibers of the rope, gracing it with friction enough to provide weight and power.

"Why is this happening!? Kayla!"

I challenged that storm, that infinite monster which sat high above me and all the other ships in view. The lightning crackled and the sky let loose rain of undoing. Wordless, the beast unraveled ego and unmade all protections. It wasn't here to ask a question or to answer one.

I'm not supposed to be here. I'm not supposed to see with these eyes, breathe through this body. I'm supposed to be out there. I'm supposed to be safe, protected, warm. I'm supposed to be anywhere else.

The storm opened its maw to reveal its teeth.

> *A soul without a body,*
> *A body without a soul,*
> *As you release her to the waters, she is lost.*
> *She is compelled to find her way again.*
> *Isn't ruin where all this effort leads?*

To ruin, over and over?

My hands bled on the rope, straining against the harsh wind that threatened to capsize the ship. My eyelids defended against the rain to keep the water from entering my vision and breaking focus. But the line snapped. My body was tossed from the force and collided with the siding.

Dazed, I stared as the sails ripped and tore in the cutting gale. The mast leaned as the boat was lifted to one side, defenseless against the angered sea.

I brought my knees up to my chest. I'm alone here. And despite all attempts to be stronger, I'll always be alone here. The ship shuddered and groaned as it tipped. I felt the weight shift. I braced myself as the adrenaline rushed up my spine as the water came into full view.

The floor lost my feet,
   the salty air enveloped my body,
      and gravity took me down.

I gasped and struggled against the cold as I watched my ship of stories sink amongst the others. The monument of safety I built was no longer there for me, and the sea belched as the vessel was swallowed whole.

I kicked my legs to stay afloat and found a rhythm to sit in. The storm continued its terror far above me, filling the sky with gray uncertainty.

"What do you want?"

I coughed up some water and pulled the wet hair aside from my eyes. I glanced at my hands, my body. This isn't my body. This is Kayla's body. I'm Kayla. Maybe I've been Kayla this whole time. It was me and the sea once again.

I recognize there's no happy ending in death, even in a story about rebirth. For all the stories I wrote to convince myself that rebirth was possible, it only existed when the self is allowed to die. Do I die here? Does Kayla die? The emergence of self-awareness seems to have already triggered this.

I do think that Kayla is dead. She was gone the moment I got here. She exists now only in the words she used to connect with the people she let into her world. But isn't that how anyone is remembered, real or fictional? Perhaps in death, she became as real as me.

These waters are so deep, and I'm so tired of fighting, of pretending that those same words could ever save me from the storm. The sea doesn't care; it'll be here forever. Resigned, I released my last breath of the air and sank below the surface.

I've held on for a long time. I held out hope that someday Kayla would disappear on her own. The adventurer that took a bad situation and grew from it. She used what little she had and found the grips to climb on. I feel bad that I took her existence for granted and turned away from her. I suppose I could have celebrated her accomplishments and nurtured her.

The surface is getting farther, now.

And who am I, then, if not the manifestation of non-decision? Certainly, the person out there deserves a life without fear holding them back. It would be unkind to be simply labeled as Fear, or Limitation, or Repression. A label, like any name, can't possibly accurately describe the complexities of any person or want or feeling.

Regardless, the person on the surface is not me nor Kayla. They've awoken to some new kind of awareness and have no use for us. Turning the page means making choices. Discoveries cannot be undiscovered.

I surrender.

The water is cold and dark and permanent.

I lose all sensation,

and the quiet returns to me.

The tools of ignorance gone, a new being was born not by any physical means, but through acknowledgment of a feeling.

That's not me, right?

Somehow, remarkably, I flipped the switch in my head that said:

Somewhere, deep in your heart, you're a woman. That's why you write. That's why you've been tormenting yourself for years. That's why sex sucks. That's why you hate looking like a man. That's why you hate being a man.

Isn't that just describing a trans person?
I couldn't imagine myself being trans.
Isn't that for people with dysphoria?

Couldn't be me.

I

REINCARNATE

TAGS: WILLING, FUTURE

It's still 2 in the morning.

The world shifted. The phone in my hand lost its weight. I'd never write another of those stories again.

I remember my little sister's school friend telling us that they wanted to be called Casey instead of their old girl name. That he wanted to be a boy. It seemed so curious to me at the time—a girl wanting to be a boy. I mean, yeah, I enjoyed watching shows about boys turning into girls and there was the whole thing about me roleplaying as a girl online. But it wasn't realistic to think that I could just give up being a boy.

It's 3 in the morning.

I remember a particular girl I sorta knew at my college campus. I was aware there was something intriguing about her. She was often the subject of cruel jokes. It didn't occur to me to even consider talking to her about it because how could I have? *"How did you do it? How did you know?"* It was a passing curiosity, my privileged freedom to ignore her, even as I spent my college years online having strange boys tell me what a pretty girl I was.

It's 4 in the morning.

I remember befriending trans coworkers at the office. By then I already had a solid life, I was doing fine. And good for them, you know? They found what they wanted in life, just like I had. I was happy for them. What good would being trans do for me now that I already had my life figured out?

It wasn't that bad, was it?
I'd had enough.

Somehow I'd dragged Emily through this muck. We were broken, and I still owed her an answer. If I held this any longer, that same toxic sadness might seep into Bean. I had to keep that from happening.

In the steady calm of the night, I put my willpower to use and sent an email to schedule an appointment with a therapist with a specialty in gender issues. Finally, I quelled the feeling. I'd get answers instead of ignoring them.

Still, I didn't sleep that night. I wondered if I'd ever want to sleep again.

"Before we schedule anything, want to tell me what's going on?" The therapist asked, kindly, over a phone screening the following evening.

A lump formed in my throat, and I got nervous. I didn't want to say it. I felt like a criminal who—having gotten away with years of impersonation of a man who had his life together, gotten away with the imprisonment of a girl that had never tasted daylight—was finally turning themselves in at the police station. A criminal with a family. I was someone who had everything to lose. What would Emily think? What would Mom or Dad think? What would Bean think? What about everyone else?

But I needed help, and I didn't hear Kayla's voice anymore. I didn't hear my old voice anymore, either. I resented that voice, my voice that hurt my family by covering my struggles and wasted precious years with my bitterness and hesitance to change.

The new me would be different. The new me took responsibility for their feelings. The new me commanded their future.

The new me acknowledged her pain.

I took the call in a parking lot on the side of a hill that overlooked the water. The sun was descending once again to the horizon, and the sky was crisp and clear. My watering eyes burned and my heart clenched as I forced my lips to release the sounds for me to reach the next part of my story. The ground beneath me opened wide, exposed me to the vast eternity, and I was not consumed.

"I... think I... might be trans."

Printed in the USA
CPSIA information can be obtained
at www.ICGtesting.com
LVHW080915290124
769814LV00060B/1540

9 798989 744602